An Honorable Viscount

Of Valor and Honor, Book 2

By

Jessica A. Clements

© Copyright 2023 by Jessica A. Clements
Text by Jessica A. Clements
Cover by Kim Killion

Dragonblade Publishing, Inc. is an imprint of Kathryn Le Veque Novels, Inc.
P.O. Box 23
Moreno Valley, CA 92556
ceo@dragonbladepublishing.com

Produced in the United States of America

First Edition October 2023
Trade Paperback Edition

Reproduction of any kind except where it pertains to short quotes in relation to advertising or promotion is strictly prohibited.

All Rights Reserved.

The characters and events portrayed in this book are fictitious. Any similarity to real persons, living or dead, is purely coincidental and not intended by the author.

ARE YOU SIGNED UP FOR DRAGONBLADE'S BLOG?

You'll get the latest news and information on exclusive giveaways, exclusive excerpts, coming releases, sales, free books, cover reveals and more.

Check out our complete list of authors, too!

No spam, no junk. That's a promise!

Sign Up Here

www.dragonbladepublishing.com

Dearest Reader;

Thank you for your support of a small press. At Dragonblade Publishing, we strive to bring you the highest quality Historical Romance from some of the best authors in the business. Without your support, there is no 'us', so we sincerely hope you adore these stories and find some new favorite authors along the way.

Happy Reading!

CEO, Dragonblade Publishing

Additional Dragonblade books by Author Jessica Clements

Of Valor and Honor Series
The Scottish Duke (Book 1)
An Honorable Viscount (Book 2)

Prologue

June 15, 1815, the Battle of Waterloo

JAMES HAD GOTTEN the news that Napoleon was on the move just days before at the most sought-after fete on the Continent. He had been dancing away the hours with all the ladies in attendance, drinking copious amounts of wine, and visiting with his friends.

Looking back on that day, he should have spent more time with his men. Yet, again, he didn't know what he would go through later in the week.

James's breath hitched when another volley of musket fire barraged on his position. He couldn't fire back, his ammunition spent minutes before. He had scavenged what remained from his dead friends, hoping to find enough to push the French bastards back.

The battlefield surrounded him. The smoke hung heavy over the land. He couldn't hold back the coughs that racked his body. The coppery scent of blood mixed with the acrid scent of the smoke was almost too much to bear. He surveyed the carnage around him. Sightless eyes beckoned him to continue the assault on the Frenchmen. The maimed and wounded begged him to help them escape the pain or for him to carry them to the field hospital.

He would never forget what he saw around him. There was

nothing he could do for them—not a thing. He shook his head in dismay. Except for some luck, he would have been in the same condition as the men around him. His friend Neil had stepped between him and a bullet that had his name on it. The young private that stood behind James at the beginning of the battle had lost his life during the first wave.

Another volley broke him out of his thoughts. He surveyed around him again. *Damn and blast!* He was well in front of the lines, within range of the long-distance artillery. A *BOOM!* rang out in the distance. He had trained for moments such as this, but his mind went blank.

James watched as the ball arched and landed feet away from him, blowing him backward. Earth, wood, and shrapnel hit him and any man in its path. He cringed as he hit the ground at the top of the crater that the ball made in the muddy field. He felt himself rolling and the world went dark.

FOR A MOMENT, James opened his eyes as he felt himself being dragged somewhere. The silence around him meant one thing—the battle was over. Yet the smells assaulted him, making him wish that he had not woken up. He cataloged his injuries as he cursed the man who was dragging him. He was sure that he had a massive bump on his head. He was also sure that he had a broken leg, and copious amounts of shrapnel lodged in places he never wanted to think about.

James glanced up at the man who was dragging him. He looked familiar, but James couldn't place him. He couldn't think with all the pain he was in. He could barely remember his own name, let alone someone else's.

It wasn't the pain he would remember in the years to come, but the words that his rescuer spoke.

"You are going to do important work in the coming years.

The Crown and the British people will need you. Unfortunately, our path ends here," the man told him.

James heard feet trudging toward him. Whoever they were jostled him as they slid him onto a litter. As the men carried him toward the field hospital, James looked around him, and then the black shadows took over. He closed his eyes, succumbing to the pain.

Chapter One

London, many months later

JAMES KIRBY, THE new Viscount Riverton, sat behind his desk at Kirby and Son's Shipping. He had taken over the shipping company after his father died and just before he bought his commission into the Royal Dragoons—before the Battle of Waterloo, where he was gravely injured.

The memories of that day were fuzzy, to say the least, but he did remember waking up at the field hospital as the doctors were trying to get all the shrapnel out of his body. Then there was nothing until he woke up on a ship bound for London.

James shook his head and stared at his account book. He had been going over the same column of numbers for too long, and it rankled him. He recognized the date, the day the Valor and Honor men went to Edinburgh to find a killer. He knew he would be floating the cost of the trip but didn't consider the amount of food that they went through on the voyage. He had the money to spend, but for official duties—it should be able to be billed to Whitehall. Maybe Lady Rosemont would know.

The Valor and Honor Investigators started as an investigative arm of Tarleton's office at Whitehall. Instead of information gathering, like Tarleton's spies, the investigators stuck closer to home. They looked into murders, lost or stolen jewelry, and abductions. Their first case was the assassination of the old Duke of Rathdrum and his three elder sons. The youngest son, the new Duke of Rathdrum, was the leader of the group. They still had not unraveled all the threads of the murders, but James knew that something would give soon.

James glanced over at the clock on the mantel. Ioan, one of his closest friends and leader of Valor and Honor Investigative Services, had set a meeting at Rathdrum House in Mayfair. They had an ongoing case that involved the deaths of Ioan's family—and the disappearance of a young man on the Continent.

If he was going to make it on time, James knew that he would have to leave as soon as he could. But with his leg causing him issues, his normal form of transportation was out of the question. Sitting on a horse as a sliver of shrapnel pushed its way out of his leg wasn't enjoyable in the least.

James strode out of the shipping office, locked the door behind him, and climbed into the waiting carriage.

"Rathdrum House," he told his driver, and he rapped his walking stick on the ceiling of the carriage as he settled into the plush seats of the conveyance.

The carriage jostled him as he struggled to keep his seat. Once he gained purchase, he rubbed his leg, feeling the jagged edge of a metal shard pierce the skin. Thank God he didn't have far to go. If he needed it, Ioan always kept a room waiting for him in cases like this. His friend had been with him during his not-so-easy recovery.

The journey from his offices to Mayfair gave him time to think. Jeffers, the former butler at Ioan's Scottish estate, turned out to be Ioan's bastard uncle. That last revelation had come as a shock to all the men and women who witnessed the apprehension of the scoundrel. Now, the man was on his way to Australia.

James couldn't stop wondering about that trip. The ship, one of his own, had not sent word back to England in far too long. Of course, the only way to get word back was another ship. And he had no other ships in the area that he knew of. It was too late to send another ship out for this matter. Nonetheless, he would have to await word and go back through his records to see if he had any ships coming back from Australia to watch out for the *Nautilus*. He would investigate it in the morning.

He watched while the sun dropped below the buildings as the carriage made its way through the maze of streets. If he were to be honest with himself, he missed the structured existence of being in the dragoons. He missed his time at sea. He missed Scotland.

Finally, several minutes later, he noticed the façade of the ducal manse and thanked God that he had gotten there with no mishap. He would talk with Elijah, physician for Tarleton turned friend of the Valor and Honor Investigators, about his injuries once he got into the house—if he could make it up the stairs.

James knew that he would have to deal with the pain for the rest of his life. At least the doctors were able to save his leg—and for that he would be eternally grateful. Yet a part of him couldn't help but wonder if his life would be easier if the doctors had taken his leg. He stretched the limb as the carriage came to a halt.

James alighted feeling stiff and achy. He held himself up with his walking stick that he kept in his carriage just in case this happened. He leaned heavily on the cane as he made his way up the stairs and into his friend's home.

FROM INSIDE THE house, Silas watched as the man he'd saved on a faraway battlefield struggled to make it up the stairs of the Duke of Rathdrum's townhouse. Silas remembered his final words on the battlefield to—now—his friend. He'd had to eat his words because they did, in fact, meet again. At first, Silas, had been tasked to keep the man alive because the Priest had wanted Riverton for his own nefarious reasons. To be honest, he hadn't been sure that the man would make it out of surgery. The field hospital was a deplorable place on the best of days. After a horrible battle, the place was knee deep in shoes with feet still in them.

Over the last couple of months, Silas had gotten to know Riverton, and he had never been happier that he had saved the man's life at Waterloo. He secretly hoped that his brother would be able to work his magic on Riverton. Sooner or later, the man would have to ask.

"Sir, the Viscount Riverton is here to see you," a footman announced.

Me? Why me? Why not Elijah?

"Very well. I will see him here." Silas nodded his thanks to the footman.

Silas stared at Riverton as he maneuvered around the chairs and tables of the parlor, limping as he went.

"Having a bad day with the leg?"

"Does it look like I'm having a bad day?" Riverton grumpily replied.

Silas raised his hands in surrender. "I saw you climbing those stairs, and my own legs hurt watching you. Have you spoken to Elijah about your leg?"

"I was going to tonight. But I needed to rest, and then I felt like speaking with you while waiting for the meeting."

Silas nodded. It was apparent to him that Riverton needed someone to talk with about his time at Waterloo, and since Silas was there—why not? "You know that you can talk to me about anything."

Riverton turned a seething glance at him. "I would rather keep that time of my life to myself. Those are memories I would not like to speak about."

Silas understood. He had memories of the battle that he never wanted to dredge up. Just thinking of that day had him flashing back to the bloody field. He had to stop thinking about it or he would be in a very bad place, very quickly.

"I see that you wouldn't want to speak about your experience at Waterloo either," Riverton continued. "When you decide to rehash your experiences, I will do the same. Until then, I would like to imagine that my leg isn't useless and my temper can be wrangled by the strength of my will." He chuckled.

Silas contemplated what the viscount said. The man clearly was in pain, excruciating pain. "I know Elijah is in his office down the hall. I think it may be worth a visit."

Riverton nodded and proceeded to pull himself up and limp from the room, leaving Silas to the mercy of his memories.

He was constantly reminded of the atrocities of war. One moment he would be in a conversation, the next he was cowering under a desk. The cannons firing, the horrendous sound of when the ball landed, the screams of the men that it encountered on its path of destruction—he could see and hear it as if it was happening in front of him all over again, the battle playing out in his dreams. After speaking with many former soldiers, he knew that they never came back the same. They left a part of their minds behind on that bloody battlefield.

Silas shook his head, bringing him back to the present. He needed to force these episodes back so his brother didn't lock him up in Bedlam. He wouldn't, or couldn't, blame Elijah for doing it, but he had much he needed to do before then.

Chapter Two

JAMES BARELY MADE it to Elijah's room without succumbing to the pain in his injured leg. He crashed into the doctor's door just as Elijah opened it and helped him into his lair. He had been to Elijah's office many times in the last several months, every time feeling the shrapnel still making its way out of his body.

"I'm assuming the reason why you are crashing into my office is because of your leg. You should've really come to me before you got to this point, my friend," Elijah stated as he kneeled next to James.

"It wasn't paining me much until I had to climb the stairs up to the door. Why does there always have to be stairs?" James focused his wrath on each word.

"James, by the evidence I see, you have been in pain much longer than the couple of minutes you've been here at Rathdrum House. You're pale, sweating, and in a great deal of pain. You, my friend, have been lying to yourself. Let me look at the leg."

In his pain-numbed mind, he made out the doctor's words but couldn't get his body to cooperate. "I need help, Elijah—" he barely heard himself say.

"*Damn!*" He heard the doctor bellow that he needed more people in the room, then his vision dimmed and everything went black.

WHEN JAMES WOKE, the pain was slightly better. He reached down and felt the bare skin of his leg. Where were his trousers? That bastard better not have cut him from his boots and trousers, damn it! He opened his eyes and surveyed the room. In a chair near the bed in which he currently resided, there was a stack of clothing. Tucked near the chair were his boots. He sighed in relief.

"You're awake!" A female voice he assumed was Matilda rang throughout the room. "You worried us, James."

He blinked and stared into the eyes of his friend's wife. Matilda was a little pixie of a woman who clearly had nothing better to do than watch over him.

"I know where that mind of yours wandered off to, James. I had plenty of other things I could have done, but your friends are worried about you. You never complain of the pain you're constantly in. When you collapsed…" She sniffled.

Why did women have to cry over the smallest things? James put his hand over hers. "I will be up and about in no time. There is too much to be done and not enough men, and women, to do it. I need to get up."

"No, you don't. You've been delirious for several days. Your leg is still healing." Matilda glanced over at the door. "I will be back. I need to let Elijah know that you are awake."

"Are you certain? Several days? What day is it?" His scrambled thoughts voiced themselves all at once.

"It's Sunday, James."

James nodded. Inside, he knew that Matilda was right. He was weakened by the shock that his body went through.

"It's about bloody time you opened those eyes," the Scottish brogue of his longtime friend Ioan said from the door.

"I'm so glad I could oblige you." James chuckled.

"Obliging me, my arse. You scared everyone. You should've

really had the surgeon at Waterloo cut off that damn leg." Ioan sat in a chair next the bed.

"If I had lost my leg, I wouldn't be able to do half the things I'm able to do now. I need to be able to sit on a horse, climb stairs, and walk with ease. I can't lose my leg, Ioan. I didn't want to lose it then, and I sure as hell am not going to lose it now."

"I am not suggesting having Elijah remove the leg," Ioan replied. "I promise. It would have been kinder for the battle surgeon to do the deed. Since he did not, you are stuck in the position you are in."

"I apologize for my surly temper. Tell me, how did the meeting go?" James asked his friend. Hopefully, deflecting the subject would help him rein in his temper.

Ioan frowned at him before replying. "Tarleton needs to find the person behind the Shadows, this Priest. He thinks that the Priest is behind the murder of my family—a sanctioned assassination."

James took a moment to ponder that. "Do you think that the Priest is close to you? That he knew your father and brothers?"

"Logic says yes. Since my illegitimate uncle was part of the whole plot..." Ioan's voice faded. "Speaking of which, have you heard anything about the ship?"

James shook his head but quickly stopped when the room started to spin around him. "No, nothing. My ship should be halfway to Australia by now, I would imagine. I have no other ships in the area. Anything could have happened to the ship and I wouldn't know it. They should be at the dock in the next couple of weeks. We should know something in a couple of months." James shrugged.

Dismay spread across Ioan's face and into his eyes. "So much could happen between here and there. I know I should've just killed the man."

James could empathize. They had been close friends and neighbors for years before he or Ioan came into their titles. He was just as much part of Ioan's family as Ioan was. It angered him that the butler at Ioan's Scottish estate—Rathdrum Hall—had been an agent for a rival spy network, known as the Shadows—and they later found out that the butler was the bastard brother of Ioan's father.

"If you did, you would be in the same position as you are now, but with blood on your hands. If only we could get news sooner." James sighed heavily.

"I think we all do. In the meantime, Tarleton has me going through the family records for a project. I will go get Elijah; he was worried about you."

At that moment, the room started spinning again. "Please send him in," James was barely able to instruct Ioan before everything went dark—again.

TARLETON—THE SPYMASTER AND Matilda's maternal uncle—had waited in the parlor, along with the other Valor and Honor investigators, for word of how Riverton was doing. Percy, his brother by marriage and Matilda's father, was also sitting in the parlor, fingers steepled beneath his chin. Over the years, a friendship, born of duty, had resulted in a mutual understanding between the two men. Wherever Tarleton went, Percy went too.

"You're planning something?" Percy asked.

"What gave you that idea?" Tarleton replied. He knew that it angered Percy when he replied with a question. Percy claimed that it was rude and counterproductive.

"You know I despise when you do that. What do you have planned?" Percy asked.

"Margaret."

"Oh. What are you going to do with her?" Percy's quizzical look surprised Tarleton.

"If you remember, Lady Margaret Stapleton was the fiancée to the eldest of Rathdrum's brothers. When he was murdered,

Margaret asked for more intense missions. What if I put her and Riverton together to solve the riddle of who the Priest is and who murdered Ioan's family?" Tarleton mumbled.

"Are you trying your hand at matchmaking? Now that you're happy and nearly wed, you want everyone else to be just as happy."

Tarleton chuckled, which was not like him at all, but he would acknowledge his need to lighten the spirits of those around him. The Valor and Honor men needed happiness as much as they needed a good riddle to solve.

Percy rolled his eyes. "I knew it. Don't think about finding me a match. The love of my life was taken from me years ago."

Tarleton cocked an eyebrow. "Are you adamant about that? You know I will take that as a challenge. My sister would not have wanted you to go through life without happiness. I just might find someone for you yet."

A door opening and hurried footsteps indicated that Ioan was heading in their direction. Tarleton stood and adjusted his waistcoat as he waited for the approaching duke. Once Ioan sat down in one of the many chairs in the room, Tarleton once again sat in the chair he had just vacated.

"Well, how is he?" Tarleton asked his niece's husband.

"He is better. The fever has broken, but he is still very weak. It will be a fortnight before he will be able to do more than walk about the grounds," Ioan replied, raking his fingers through his hair.

"I may have just the thing," Tarleton said. "It was a brilliant idea to move your family's records to London. I'm sure we could find something on the Priest or even your bastard uncle. I also have another agent between missions who may be able to help in that regard."

"Uncle Anthony, you aren't trying to matchmake, are you?" Matilda glided into the room in a beautiful emerald-green dress with a lighter green overdress.

"Would I ever do such a thing?" Tarleton replied, pretending to be admonished.

"I know you, Uncle. Who is it you are going to put together?" Matilda put her hands on her hips and stared at him.

Tarleton couldn't help but smile. His niece reminded him so much of his late sister. He loved seeing her so happy with her duke. He thought for a moment before replying.

"Margaret Stapleton needs a new project before she starts causing trouble again. I thought I would partner her with Riverton."

"James? With Margaret? Oh, Uncle Anthony, trouble would be the least of your worries." Matilda's eyes twinkled.

"I understand the implications of what I'm planning, dear niece. Either they will work together or they will murder each other in broad daylight. Or there is another option—they fall in love and live happily ever after." Tarleton pushed himself out of his chair, strode over to his niece, and took her hands. "Just leave it to me." He winked before walking out of the room.

Now, he had to find Margaret. The woman never stayed in one place long. The half-Irish, half-English beauty would be causing trouble with the priests at Saint George's. She always had something to bring up about their theology. Knowing her as he did, he knew that Maggie would be storming across the pavilion sooner rather than later. He strode toward the mews to get his horse and, hopefully, get to Saint George's before the whole of London knew what the woman was capable of.

LADY MARGARET STAPLETON sat on the steps of Saint George's after being bodily thrown from the massive church. She couldn't blame the priests. She was the devil incarnate to them. Margaret had learned her mother's Irish ways. No, not the Catholic way, but the old ways. Her mother had passed down the religion of her forefathers. A religion not spoken about in mixed company.

The archbishop wanted nothing to do with her. It was probably why he'd never granted a special license for her and her late fiancé. She shrugged to herself. She supposed she could keep her dislike of the English church to herself because she worked for the Crown.

Who needs priests, anyway? she asked herself. To be certain, she didn't.

She huffed a sigh as she watched a tall man on a horse amble toward her. She recognized the man. *Damn and blast,* she swore to herself.

"Did they have enough of you?" Tarleton asked as he drew his horse to a stop.

"Would I be out here sitting on this marble step if they hadn't?" She pushed herself from the step.

"What did you debate this time?"

Maggie teetered back and forth on her feet and quickly glanced away from the spymaster. "Well, I would rather…um…not say," she mumbled.

Tarleton guffawed before sliding from his horse. "One of these days, they will do something about your insolence. Please be careful. I don't want you going to your grave a head short."

Shocked at the spymaster's words, Maggie turned away from him. "If I die, it won't be at the hands of the church but on the Continent after a mission gone bad." *Well, this conversation certainly turned morbid rather quickly.* "Are you going to help me home, or am I stuck here until morning?"

She couldn't help but berate herself for sounding so childish. She was far away from her lodgings and the only place remotely close was Rathdrum House, and she couldn't assume that they would allow her through the door.

"You should have become an actress, my dear. You know you are welcome at my niece's house. She would, more than likely, commandeer you for a small recital. Now, let's go so the archbishop doesn't have a seizure when he finds you still on his doorstep in the morning." Tarleton guided his horse toward

Maggie and helped her to sit on the beast.

"It has been a while since I've seen Ioan or Matilda, for that matter. It may do my heart some good," Maggie said to herself, just loud enough for Tarleton to hear.

She glanced down at the spymaster from her perch on the horse. It hadn't been too long ago that she had felt lost. Her fiancé had been murdered, her own family had disowned her—for which she didn't have an answer—and the only person she trusted was standing next to her. He had been a close family friend, and when her whole world crashed around her, he'd picked her up and given her purpose.

"If you want to spend the night on the steps of Saint George's, that's up to you. I am going to find my way back to Rathdrum House."

She knew what Tarleton was up to. The manipulative man knew how to push the right buttons to get her to do what he wanted. "Lead the way, my lord," she squeaked out as the horse began to move.

"Please be careful with how far you hassle the bishops and priests. I would rather you needle the *ton* then poke fun at those who could have you put to death," Tarleton whispered in her ear.

Maggie knew that he spoke the truth. Damn the man. "Well, let's go. I am rather hungry, now that I think about it. I could raid the duke's larder."

It was a blessing to her ears when she heard Tarleton's laugh from behind her. It had been too long since she had heard it, and it took her to a better time in her life. She continued to listen to the laughter as she rode the horse and Tarleton guided them toward Rathdrum House.

Chapter Three

Somewhere in the Atlantic Ocean

CAPTAIN PHILIP MAYHEW, of the *Fury*, was rethinking his life decisions after firing on the English vessel heading toward Australia. The man that he had taken from the English was not someone he was proud to know. He knew that he owed the man a significant amount of money, and for that, he had only himself to blame.

Philip shook his head. He was an American privateer. He would much rather run down pirates than be called one, but if the shoe fit... The bastard had called in his debt. Philip clenched his teeth and felt himself shake in anger.

He could still mentally slap himself for his moment of weakness during a game of whist. He'd never let it happen again. To this day, he had not touched a dram of whiskey or rum because of the events that led to this mission.

The blue sky above him gave way to gray on the horizon. A storm would be brewing by supper. It would be just Philip's luck. The next port was still weeks away, so finding an inland harbor or a protected inlet would be hard if he wanted to stay away from possible pirate strongholds, of which there were plenty.

"Captain?" Jeffers's annoying voice came from his cabin.

"What can I do for you?" Philip harshly asked.

"I would watch your tone if I were you. I may not know how

to sail a ship, but I do know how to incite a riot. You know what that means onboard a ship," Jeffers threatened.

Philip was in a position that he didn't like one bit. On one hand, he could tell the other man to mind his words—which wouldn't go over well, because no captain of a ship wanted a mutiny. On the other hand, if he kept his mouth shut, he was doomed to do as Jeffers asked—no matter what. The easier of the two options, for the moment, was for him to do whatever the other man asked.

"What can I do for you?" Philip repeated.

Jeffers smiled at him. "That was much better. Now, I see there is a squall coming—what are your plans to get the ship to safety?"

"I'm afraid that we don't have any protected harbors within sailing distance. We are just going to need to ride the storm out," Philip replied. It wasn't a lie—he needed to consult his charts, but Jeffers didn't need to know that.

Philip strode toward his cabin. Glancing down at the charts gave him clarity of mind, putting him back in the place where he was in charge. He would need to come up with a way to end this soon, or his life may be at risk.

MARGARET SAT AT the little writing desk in her parlor, hoping that her mistake at Saint George's hadn't ruined her chances of staying with Tarleton. She glanced down at the letter she had been writing.

She chuckled to herself. Just like the box of letters under her bed, she would never send it. Margaret would stuff the letter into the box and forget it was ever there. One day she would bury them or even burn them. Today, though, would not be that day.

She missed her family. All she had were memories. She couldn't go back now; she had changed so much in the previous years. She sniffled.

A knock on her door forced Margaret back to reality. She slowly pushed herself up from her chair and ambled toward the door, wiping away the tears that started to stream down her face.

She had an idea of who it may be—the spymaster. She rolled her eyes and reached toward the door's handle to twist it open. A whiff of cologne swept past her nose as Tarleton pushed himself into her rooms.

"Moping about, I see." The man put his hands on his hips and turned toward her.

Margaret rolled her eyes. "No, just doing some correspondence."

Tarleton guffawed. "Correspondence? Who are you corresponding with? Let's see, shall we?" He strode over to the writing desk, picked up the piece of stationery, and read out loud, "Dear Mother…"

"Stop! Please, stop. I won't ever send it. They turned their backs on me years ago; you know that. Please, just put it down." Margaret sank to the floor and bawled.

She felt warm, strong arms wrap around her. "Let it out, my dear. Let it out." Tarleton had been there when she had gotten the news that her fiancé had been murdered and when she was subsequently disinherited.

Within a couple of minutes, her tears finally stopped. "Thank you, Uncle Anthony."

"Well, I have a job for you. We need to find the Priest, the leader of the Shadows, and take him down. I need your help with that. You will be working with a Valor and Honor investigator—you must remember James Kirby?"

Margaret gasped. She knew of the man. Heir to a title and a shipping company, and handsome as sin. "Yes, I remember him. Didn't he recently inherit the title of Viscount Riverton?"

Tarleton smiled. "Yes, he did. He is friends with your late fiancé's youngest brother and is one of the founding members of Valor and Honor Investigations."

It wasn't very often that she was speechless.

She rummaged through her memory for the first time she met the new Viscount Riverton. It must have been at Rathdrum Hall. She smiled. She had been there to attend a country party with her parents, just after her engagement. The younger James Kirby had been a cantankerous boy. She had been twenty-two, and James was seventeen. Five years later, she didn't know the viscount anymore.

Tarleton had a strange look on his face. "You remember that house party at Rathdrum Hall. I was there too with your parents and the previous Duke of Rathdrum. James was smitten with you then."

Margaret gasped. "You better not be trying to matchmake for me, Uncle Anthony. If I wanted a husband, I would already be married."

"I will remember you said that, my dear. You will be working with him on this mission. You aren't my only contact that I will be reaching out to in order to bring this man down. There is another spy network, and the leader is a friend of mine. You may remember that the former Duke of Rathdrum and his three elder sons were part of an inherited spy group?"

"I remember. The Rakes, am I correct?"

"Yes, they were on loan to me to search for a young man, and I needed their expertise—and their records."

Well, that made sense to a small degree. Tarleton was calling in his markers with other networks. She knew that it would be a matter of time before they had their man. Though she knew this mission may be fraught with horrible twists and turns. This wasn't going to be over quickly.

"Very well, I will do this for you. When do I start?" Margaret asked.

"I will set a meeting with Riverton for tomorrow. I would like you to be there."

"Yes, sir," she replied.

Margaret watched as Tarleton strode out of the room.

Chapter Four

Early the next morning, James stretched in his bed. He'd had the worst night so far. Not that his leg was giving him problems. Not at all. There weren't any shards of metal actively trying to force their way through his skin, though he knew there were still shards left in his leg. It was the dreams that had woken him periodically throughout the night. He'd watched repeatedly as his friends were maimed and killed on the battlefield.

Like every morning, James got ready for the day. Today he had a morning sojourn with Tarleton. James had been given the job of continuing to find out the truth about the deaths of Ioan's family. He would need to go to the record room now at Ioan's townhouse—Rathdrum House.

He was seated at the large table in the dining room, sipping on a steaming cup of tea, when Tarleton was announced. James glanced over at the clock mounted on the wall not far from him. Tarleton was nothing if not punctual. He couldn't help but chuckle.

James put his hands down on the chair, ready to push himself up to stand, but was stayed by the spymaster.

"No need to get up, Riverton," Tarleton said as he sat down in the chair next to James.

"My lord, a Lady Margaret Stapleton is here. Shall I escort her here or to your office?" a footman asked.

Lady Margaret Stapleton? It couldn't be. The woman James was smitten with years ago. Ioan's eldest brother's fiancée. God Almighty, could his day get any more complicated? He went through his day up to this point: nightmares, Lady Margaret Stapleton, the damn spymaster—what more could this day give him? And it was only breakfast!

"Show her here. Oh, and John, please bring more refreshments for our guests." James waved the footman to do his bidding. He wasn't indifferent to his staff; they had been more like family since his own family—

He shouldn't have thought of that.

Moments later, Lady Margaret stepped into the room, and James's mouth went dry. She was more beautiful now than when he first met her.

"My lady, it is a pleasure to have you here." James smiled, gesturing his guest to take a seat.

"Tarleton, what is this meeting about?" she said.

"I need your help. Not only do we need to find the Priest, but we need to find a missing heir. My men are spread thin on the Continent. I need to utilize investigators—you—to find these people." Tarleton continued to watch James eat his breakfast.

James nodded. "I understand the mission, but why are we having this meeting while I'm breaking my fast? Please, enjoy some of Cook's pastries. They are the best—outside of France, that is."

The quizzical look coming from Lady Margaret stumped him. Her being here at his table let him know that she worked for Tarleton in some way. But in what capacity? He couldn't think about that now. He had too much on his plate. A mission from Tarleton could kill him—figuratively. He could feel the weight of the world on his shoulders, and it wasn't a good feeling to have.

MARGARET GLANCED OVER at Riverton. The man was even more

mouth-wateringly gorgeous than she remembered him as a boy. Goodness! His shoulders were wide, his arms muscular and defined, his short sable hair was fashionable—Adonis had nothing on him. She felt her lips form a smile. But she had a job to do, a mission to complete—she didn't have time for a liaison or a brief affair.

She turned toward Tarleton, who was smiling. Damn the man! He was matchmaking. This would never work, never. Yet she had a feeling that Tarleton knew what he was doing. James was the opposite of her in every way possible. He was grounded, owned a successful shipping company, and was richer than her father—many times over.

She was the disinherited child of an earl, who became a spy when her fiancé was murdered—well, that had not been proved, yet. She was five years older than the enigmatic viscount, and she would never be able to live with herself if she became infatuated with the man.

Shaking her head, Margaret turned toward the dishes set out on the table for breakfast. Her mouth watered when she saw her favorite pastry on a tray in front of her.

"You can have one if you wish, my lady," Riverton said.

The man's voice gave her goosebumps. There was something about his bass voice that resonated through her. "Thank you, my lord," she managed to reply as she reached for the pastry.

She glanced over to Tarleton, who looked like the cat who stole the cream, and wished that the meeting would begin already.

"Seeing as my protégée is secretly hoping this meeting will commence, I believe it is time to talk about why we are here," Tarleton started. "We need to find the Priest. I know you've heard this a lot in the last couple of months, as he is wanted for the death of three peers of the realm. We also need to find out what Rathdrum knew before he was murdered. It may lead us to the next clue. I have a feeling that the man is someone we know. Also, I have contacts within the inherited spy network known as the Rakes, and the Crown. They will be sending one of theirs to help with our mission."

"Why are we bringing in another group when we can hire more investigators?" James asked. "We still have the remaining men from my battalion who are in the middle of their training as we speak. They are ready to help us."

Margaret knew that the conversation could get heated quickly. The James she knew had not been quick to anger. Though time had changed the boy into a man—and war had changed him too. The innocent boy she had known had turned into a hardened soldier with a grudge against the world.

Tarleton sighed. "You can send your men out on assignment, but you need someone who knows about what my men were looking for before they died. I believe that the Rakes's leader will be sending over the Duke of Dunsbury and his wife, Juliana. I know that you are acquainted with them."

Margaret did know Juliana. The code breaker was nearly as good as Matilda. Juliana had been her friend when she had no one. Well, she could say the same about Matilda. "I didn't realize you were bringing Marcus and Juliana into this. I don't think that would be the best of plans."

"Juliana may be with child, but I have it on good authority that she is one of the best code breakers, and Marcus is just as good. If Matilda wasn't working on something else, she would've been my first choice for this assignment."

Margaret nodded. There was always a logical reason behind Tarleton's way of thinking.

"While Juliana tries to break the code, I need you and Margaret to sift through Rathdrum's records to see what his father and brothers may have found," he continued.

"I seem to be a bit confused. Why are there two people working on that assignment? Surely one person is enough." James scowled at the spymaster.

"I have my reasons. There are a lot of records to go through. If you were wondering, Matilda is deciphering the coded notes that the previous Rathdrum left behind."

Well, Matilda was the best at ciphers and codes in England. The woman was brilliant, talented, and utterly astonishing. Margaret was constantly surprised by her talent. Which reminded her, she need to visit Matilda soon. She had a desire to sing a special song that she had just heard, and hoped that her friend knew the song. Margaret continued daydreaming as the meeting went on without her.

Chapter Five

LILY THOMPSON STRODE through the busy streets of London, hoping for the best in a bad situation. Her family had fallen on hard times, and it was up to her to get work. Her father had been injured at the Battle of Waterloo, and her older brother had died during the same battle, which left her and her mother—who was heavy with child—to bring food to the table.

She searched her memories for the day she took the job for the church. At some point, she would have done anything for the church. Now, though, she was having second thoughts about what she did. The bishop that she worked for was up to no good, but she needed the money. Lily was a carrier. She slipped messages in holes in the trees or walls. She had been trained to be a pickpocket so that she could slide a message into a person's pocket without them knowing. She was good at what she did.

She was on her way to Saint George's when an acquaintance stopped her.

"I haven't seen you in a while, Lily. Are you well?" Margaret asked her.

"I am well. I've been working more than usual. My mother is heavy with child and can't work until after the babe is born. That's what Doctor Elijah told her." Lily smiled at her friend.

"Hopefully, once the babe is born, things won't be so bad."

"I certainly hope so. It was a pleasure to see you, but I have an appointment I am late for." Lily looked sheepishly toward the ground.

"If you need anything, you'll let me know?" Margaret asked.

Lily nodded as she raced toward Saint George's.

"You are *late!*" roared the man that she worked for.

"I—"

"There are no excuses. I had messages for you to deliver, and you weren't here. Now, get dressed."

Since Lily was a woman, she had to dress in boys' clothes to disguise who she was. She strode into a small closet where her clothes were hidden and began her transformation. She always started by binding her breasts. It wasn't like she was bountiful in that area, but she had enough for someone to notice. Dressed as a boy, she had more freedom.

As she left the closet, she saw a small platter on the desk in front of her that held the missives that she needed to deliver. She knew where they were meant to go—secret hiding places in the mantels of fireplaces, holes in tree trunks, under a rock in a garden. She had delivered many letters to the same secret places over the last several months.

She glanced up when she heard a door snick.

"My dear, I have a very special missive I need you to deliver today, along with the other messages. These need to go down to the docks to the quartermaster's office. You do know where it is?"

Of course she knew where the quartermaster's office was— not far from the office of the Viscount Riverton's shipping company. She had followed the news sheets about the viscount and his friends. She thought they were dashing and heroically honorable.

Shame penetrated her thoughts. Lily had thought that what *she* did was honorable when she started this job. Unfortunately, she no longer knew if it was.

There was no going back. She would need to finish this, but maybe the Viscount Riverton would like to know what was happening under his nose. Lily knew that her life was at risk if she went to the viscount. Overall, it would be worth the cost to get her family out of the clutches of a madman.

A COUPLE DAYS after the meeting with Tarleton, James sat in his office at the docks. The boat that had transported Jeffers to Australia was scheduled to return in a couple of days. Other ships would have been in the same general area and would've been able to make contact. Yet there was nothing. He supposed that it was his lucky that day he had not put actual cargo on the ship. He would have to assume that the ship went down in the traitorous waters at the Horn of Africa, or maybe due to pirates.

He went back over his books and could make out no numbers or letters. He would have to have Lizzy look at them. James knew that he was a decent hand at mathematics, but his own printing was beyond what he was able to read now. He sighed in disbelief. He had been doing the ledger for the shipping company his father gave to him for completing his schooling. He had high marks in mathematics, Latin, and history. He couldn't get enough of learning how the company worked, how he could make money from it. With Ioan's acumen for the markets, he was able to make the shipping company profitable in a short amount of time.

Yet his mind wasn't on the books or ledgers. It was on Margaret Stapleton. She had gotten lovelier since he had last seen her. He had a hard time not thinking about her. God! He needed to get his mind in the game. Or he would be seen with a massive bump in his britches. He had to laugh at that to himself.

Joshua, his assistant at the shipping company, ran through the door.

"Sir! We have news on the ship, sir!" Joshua had a bubbly personality that he couldn't seem to let go of. He strode over to James's desk and handed him the missive. James opened the note and gasped. A privateer ship had declared war on his little schooner and sent her to Davy Jones's locker. Damn it! He couldn't understand. Though he had somehow known that Jeffers had gotten help from the privateer before he turned himself in.

"Our ship is no longer," James said to Joshua. "We need to get word to Rathdrum and Phineas. They will need to know."

Joshua nodded as he ran from the room to put pen to foolscap to get a message to James's friends. He would need to tell Tarleton, also. Fuck! He couldn't admit to himself that he had lost a prisoner and a ship all at once. He shook his head and thought that maybe, just maybe, he would be able to save the day.

Just as James was about to leave his office, a whirlwind of a woman barged through his door.

"What are you doing here?" he asked Margaret as she found her way through to his office.

"I heard from your assistant, as he barreled through the door, that your ship had been fired upon and the prisoner escaped." She sounded like she had rehearsed her speech.

"Why did he tell you this? I don't know why he would tell you—but yes, our ship that held Jeffers was lost," he ground out through clenched teeth.

"It sounds as if you need my help. It's a good thing that I was on my way here anyway. I came upon a close friend as I was walking here. I have reason to believe that she is in trouble. I know what a troubled person looks like, and I can't help but say that—if we can help her, we need to help her."

James didn't know why she was telling him this, but if the girl needed help, he could give her a job in his office.

"I want to know what I can do," James demanded.

"She is in a tough spot. Elijah has been to see her mother, who is with child and isn't doing well. Her eldest child already passed away at Waterloo, and her husband was horribly injured in the battle."

James clenched his teeth even harder. He didn't want to think about Waterloo. His own injuries prevented him from doing some of his favorite things. They should have stopped him from riding his favorite horse, but he couldn't give up *everything*. Just thinking about riding made his leg throb in pain. He would need to have another visit with Elijah sooner rather than later.

"What do you think we can do to help her?" he asked, hoping to get a better answer than the muttered response he had gotten.

"I think it would be better for her to work for us—or Tarleton. She is working for some bishop at Saint George's. I hate that place." She cringed.

"Does this have anything to do with why Tarleton has you working with me rather than on the Continent, where you would be more useful?" James was beyond exasperated with Margaret. She may be extremely beautiful, but she had enough energy to make a young child wish for a nap.

He watched as her face dropped. Damn, he was making a fool of himself today—or maybe it was every day. He stood, brought his hand up, and caught hold of her chin to level her eyes with his.

"Margaret, you are worried for your friend, and I wish the best for her, but she will need to come to one of us for help. As to your problems with Saint George's, I am not embarrassed to be around you, but I think that Tarleton has already given you his own verbal set-down. I am not going to do that. I worry about you, my dear." He tucked a strand of her hair behind her ear and cupped her jaw with the other hand. James stared into her beautiful eyes, gauging her response to his touch.

"What do you want?" She returned his gaze as she moved her arms up his and to his shoulders.

"I would like to kiss you, my lady," James whispered into her ear. He gave her a couple of moments before he leaned down to brush his lips upon hers—and everything fell into place, like a puzzle. He couldn't explain it to himself or to anyone else.

He took another pass at her lips and groaned. He wasn't a monk by any means, but this felt too good to not go for more. He nibbled on her lower lip, hoping that she would let him in to deepen the kiss. Damn, he liked kissing her.

MARGARET COULDN'T BELIEVE what she was doing. She was kissing the viscount and enjoying every moment of it. She couldn't stop herself—she leaned into his muscular frame and kissed him back. For the love of God, she couldn't hold back. She opened for him and felt as James's tongue entered her mouth, tasting her. She moaned in pleasure as she swept her tongue along his. She couldn't understand how she couldn't have known how much she craved his touch, his kiss. Yet it had been years since they had seen each other, and that chemistry was still there.

She held back another moan. She needed to be able to be vocal. She had had relations with many men in her past, but she had never once enjoyed kissing as much as she had just now.

"Don't hold back, my lady. I want to hear your sounds, your pleasure," James whispered in her ear before trailing gentle kisses down her neck to the junction of her neck and shoulder. She couldn't, could she?

Margaret nodded. Thank God! The man pressed kisses along her jawbone to her chin and then took her mouth again. She could die tonight and die a happy woman.

As the kiss became more passionate, she couldn't imagine a better way to end a day.

Chapter Six

THE *FURY* CAME into port at Plymouth, and Jeffers was aching for a mission from his half-brother. The captain of the *Fury* had kept him on his feet with more than just a mutiny on his hands. Jeffers's brother, a bishop in London, had the pitiful captain's sweetheart in his prison—and that made him smile. Well, that and the man's brats. A loud cackle sprouted from his lungs and out into the night. That was why Jeffers had made the best of the scenario and kept his dealings to himself. He chuckled to himself. He would have to contact the Priest sooner rather than later if he wanted to live for any length of time.

He laced his fingers, brought them in front of him, and pushed out, cracking his knuckles. He was still a bit clumsy due to not having his land legs back. But he would get over that soon. He hiked his way up to the town and hailed a hackney.

"Where to, sir?" the driver asked.

"London, as soon as you can make it," Jeffers replied.

He climbed into the hackney and smiled. He knew it would take a while for them to get to London, and he also knew that he couldn't allow the driver to live. He touched the metal of the pistol that he had stuffed into his britches. He would allow his need for killing to be assuaged.

LILY HELD THE missive in her hand. Something wasn't right, and she couldn't hold back the awful feeling of... She didn't know what, but she felt the need to visit her friend Margaret. She stuffed the missive into her pocket and made her way to the big house in Mayfair that she'd witnessed her friend walking into earlier that same day. She knew not if her friend was still in the house but it was well worth a try.

When she reached the house, she pounded on the door several times before the butler made his appearance. She tried to explain who she was, but the man refused to let her enter the house. Damn him! She needed to speak with Margaret, or even someone she worked with.

There was more than one way to gain entrance into a house. She went to the side door where the servants came and went from. She slipped inside and tiptoed in the shadows, finding her way in the dark. She took her cap off her head, showing her bright red locks. She knew that Margaret would recognize her. She instinctively knew where to go—each of the townhouses on this street had the same floor plans. She needed to get to the study.

When she finally made it, the door was open. The two people inside were... Well, she didn't know what they were doing to each other, but she couldn't turn her back on the couple. After several minutes, she faked a cough and watched as they split up.

"Margaret?" She stood in the doorway, completely in shock.

"Lily?" Margaret replied. "What are you doing here?"

"I'm in trouble." Lily glanced toward the man in the room. She recognized him as the Viscount Riverton, one of her heroes. "I need help, please."

JAMES STOOD IN shock as the young woman, dressed in boys' clothing, tried desperately to keep her composure. He shook himself. He needed to get her to a chair, and quickly, before she ended up sprawled on the floor. He sprinted for her then guided her to a chair near the fireplace and pulled on the bellpull. He was thankful that his leg did well under the abuse, or he would've been the one sprawled on the floor with no way to get up.

A footman—he couldn't tell who it was from his angle—appeared at the door. "What can I get for you, my lord?"

"Some beverages for my guests, if you would, please," James replied in a clipped tone, something he tried to stop but couldn't.

The footman nodded and proceeded to the kitchens, where Cook was readying his tea. He stared up at Margaret.

"Is this the friend you were talking to me about?" he asked. His concern spiked when he saw her nod.

"I have something you need to see," the young woman replied. She rummaged around in her britches and pulled out a piece of foolscap. "You need to read it or maybe decode it; I don't know, but I was supposed to deliver this for the man who hired me."

"What is your name?" he asked politely.

"Lily, my lord," came her quiet response.

"Let me see the missive. I won't take it for long and will re-seal it after I'm done reading it. I know a woman who is very good at deciphering code—I may need to take it to her to see if she can understand it, but I won't know until I see the letter."

The young woman handed him the missive. "I wasn't planning on delivering it, my lord. I can't do this anymore. The guilt I feel… At one time, I thought I was doing good for the country. Now, I'm not so sure." She shivered enough that James could see and feel it.

"Let's get you warmed up, shall we?" He walked toward a door near the back of the study, opened it, and pulled a blanket from the small room. "There are times when I must work longer than I'm supposed to, and I stay here in my office. Or when my leg hurts too much for me to move very far, I have a small bed in there. You are more than welcome to get some rest while I find out what is in this missive."

"I can't, my lord. I need work to help my family." The girl became restless.

James mentally kicked himself. He should've remembered that her father was injured in the same battle as he. He could offer the family a place in his employ, which would include lodging, food, and income. They would be closer to Elijah, so when the babe was ready to be born, he wouldn't have to ride several miles to help the woman. Instead, he would only have to march across the street.

"I don't know what you will think about my offer, but here it goes. I am offering to hire you and your family to work in my household. Do you think that might interest your family? I provide an honest wage, housing, and food. Your mother's doctor is across the street. You don't have to accept now, but I would like you to think about it."

He watched as Lily glanced up at Margaret with hope. They held a silent conversation between the two of them. James couldn't help but slide back into a memory of him, Ioan, and Phineas in school. They never had to speak, ever. They were able to hold a conversation without speaking—just like Lily and Margaret were doing. He missed his friends. Now that Elijah was able to take more of the shrapnel out of his leg, it may be more possible for him to spend time with them.

"She will need to speak with her mother and father, but she thinks that they will agree. Is there a way that you can find her father work?" Margaret asked.

James thought for a moment. "What kind of injury does he have?"

"He lost his left arm and right leg, but he is strong. He just needs someone to see that he has worth, even though he no longer has his full body," Lily explained.

James nodded. He could find something for the man to do. Maybe a scribe? A secretary? He would have to see what the man's qualifications were. "What is your father's name?"

"Colonel Marcus Thompson." Lily's face brightened.

James felt his face lose all color, and he dropped to the floor on both knees. He couldn't escape the pain. His regiment had been next to Colonel Thompson's. More than half the other man's command had died on the battlefield. The man had been lucky by just losing some limbs.

"I fought with your father. It was an honor to serve with him." He forced a smile to his lips. He knew that his words would comfort her, but he didn't know how much he would be able to handle having her father in his house. The man was cantankerous at the very least. A total arse at best.

"Thank you, my lord. I will go now to see them. Mama will be worried that I'm not home." Lily leapt from the chair she sat in and struggled to gain her feet.

James tried to reach her before she upended herself. "Let me help you to the door, Lily."

Gratefully, the young woman took his hand and gained her feet, just as the door to the study opened and an unexpected visitor approached. Tarleton—damn it all to hell! Why was the spymaster here?

"Tarleton? What an unexpected visit." James clipped his words.

"Just making sure you are all doing what you're supposed to be doing. I see you have found a street urchin. Wait a moment. Is that Colonel Thompson's girl?" Tarleton seemed taken aback.

"Yes, my lord," she whispered.

"What are you doing in boys' clothing?" The spymaster glared at the younger woman.

"Tarleton, we will discuss her soon, but she needs to get home to her parents before the Bow Street Runners are called," James said.

He was happy to see that Tarleton was going to let the woman go. Thank God. The man was like a dog with a bone—he never let anything go, ever. For now, they needed to let Lily go home to discuss the plans with her parents.

Margaret was clearly in shock that Tarleton knew Lily or her parents. She had known that Lily's family had been prestigious once upon a time, but not so well connected that Anthony knew them. Maybe she needed some clarification.

"Uncle Anthony, what was that? You know Lily?" she asked.

"I knew her father in school. We were friends. I inherited my title as he was enlisting in the dragoons. I had a premonition about him, and all was going well. I kept an eye on the family. His son decided to go to war also but was killed at the end, at Waterloo.

"Molly was starting to show her pregnancy at that point, and Lily had picked up some odd work, doing mending and such. Then her father came back missing an arm and a leg. The money that would have come in if he could get work was not there. His elder brother, the Baron Buckley, was not in a welcoming mood when it came to his younger brother. The family had to move to the rookery."

"Couldn't they come to you?" she asked.

"Her father is very stubborn and wouldn't have taken my help," Tarleton replied.

Margaret had never known her friend like that. Damn and blast! If she had been destitute, she would've ended up in the rookeries as well. She knew what happened to women in those godforsaken hells. Tarleton had kept her from that fate and taught her to be a spy. Did he see that in Lily?

"She works for someone delivering missives—coded missives..." Margaret said.

James lifted the piece of foolscap in his hand. "We have one right here."

Margaret watched as James padded over to Tarleton and gave him the missive.

"What in the—" Tarleton roared. "Where did she get this?"

"She said that the man she works for gave it to her to deliver. She didn't know what it said, but she didn't feel right delivering it and brought it here to Margaret. What does it say?"

"They are using an old code, much easier to decipher than the newer ones. It says that our old friend Jeffers is back on English soil and he has an assassination order—and you are at the top of the list," Tarleton replied.

"It's a good thing that I earned top brass in the dragoons in marksmanship," James replied.

"I know you did, Riverton, but you are going to need an assassin. Lucky for you, you happen to be standing next to my best." Tarleton nodded toward Margaret. "She is fast and deadly. She will keep you safe."

Margaret couldn't help but snicker. She would need to grab her weapons. She was best with a pistol and knives. A musket was her least favorite, but she could kill anything she set her sights on. It had been a long time since she was picked to do this kind of mission.

"With that being said, Lily is working with our foe. Are you sure you want to bring her and her family into your fold?" Tarleton asked.

Margaret knew the answer before James uttered the words.

"Yes, I plan on bringing them here. I can give her father a job, her mother's doctor is at your fake safe house, and I can give our little messenger a better job that wouldn't scar her soul," James muttered.

Margaret had never been happier to hear James say such a thing. As soon as Tarleton left, she would make sure that James knew how she felt.

She felt her face flush and thought that Tarleton better leave quickly.

Chapter Seven

THE NEXT MORNING was a harsh one. Beyond the copious amounts of burgundy and rum that he had consumed, James knew nothing of what happened after he walked into the club. He knew the rooms, that he was in his house—in his bed. With a woman next to him? He knew that the woman, based solely on the color of her beautiful hair, was Margaret. What was she doing there? He rubbed his eyes, hoping that he was dreaming.

Damn, that must have been some night, he thought. He was shocked, though, when the spymaster barged into his rooms. The man's gaze was spitting fire at him when he noticed who was in James's bed.

"You better do right by her, Riverton," Tarleton commanded before abruptly leaving.

All James could do was nod in acquiescence. He needed to marry her. Why not? He had waited for her. He had always thought of her as his, even as a younger man. Not to say that he had been possessive over her, but he didn't know how to explain it. They just...fit. Nothing else but that.

Wasn't this how Ioan became married to Matilda? They weren't found in bed, but they were found in a bedchamber. Someone had orchestrated this scene. It wouldn't surprise him if it was Tarleton himself who did this, but something told him that it wasn't necessarily the case. But *someone* purposely tainted his drink.

A soft moan escaped Margaret's mouth as she awoke. A look of genuine terror passed through her gaze. He couldn't help but feel somehow guilty about what was about to happen. Damn whoever did this to them.

"What happened? Where am I? What are you doing here?" she asked him.

"Not so fast, darling. I can only answer one question at a time. What happened? I don't know. One minute I was a drinking a finger or two of the best whiskey from the Highlands, the next I was in bed, curled around you. Where are you? In my rooms at the townhouse. What am I doing here? Well, it is my house."

"But..."

"Tarleton has already come and gone. He has seen us in a compromising position, Maggie. I can't stop what is going to happen next." He combed his fingers through his hair.

"What do you mean?" she said in horror.

James watched as the answer flitted through her expressive eyes, and nodded. "Tarleton is rushing to the archbishop as we speak. Maybe Ioan's uncle will preside over our vows." He winked.

He heard an unladylike "hmph" come from the lady opposite him. He couldn't hold it in any longer. The loud guffaw echoed in the room. "Maggie, I think this was fate. Going back years ago, I wanted you. You were the epitome of what I was looking for in a woman. Each woman I looked at, touched, or kissed didn't quite live up to you. Please, do me the honor..."

Margaret gasped. James saw a myriad of emotions flash through her expressive eyes. He didn't know how she was going to react. He had never asked a woman to marry him. He glanced down to Margaret's eyes. "What do you say, my angel?"

He was not expecting what happened next. She rushed across the bed to him and flung herself into his arms. He wrapped his arms around her, holding her as if she might be taken away from him. In a whisper that settled in his heart and soul, the word "yes" was all he heard.

Chapter Eight

TARLETON COULDN'T STAND not knowing what was going on with his men. Well, Rathdrum's men. He couldn't find Margaret and had come across her and James cuddled together in Riverton's bed. He'd thought better of the man. Of course, Riverton hadn't always been an honorable man, but he had sure changed his life around. Tarleton knew that he would marry Margaret.

"What are you thinking about?" Tarleton's love Amelia asked from her seat in the grand library.

"I found Margaret in bed with Riverton. I do not want you to repeat that, Amy," he replied.

He knew that someday he would ask Amelia for her hand in marriage, but the ongoing mission had yet to be concluded. He wanted it completed before asking for her hand.

"Are you forcing them to wed? To be honest, I think they make a beautiful…" She gasped as Tarleton kissed her neck.

"I would step back, Tarleton. Until you put a ring on her finger, there will be no funny business, and I know you understand what I mean," Amelia's brother Silas said from the opposite corner, acting as her chaperone.

Tarleton nodded and replied, "They will be wed in the morning by Rathdrum's uncle, the bishop. Now, let's get to more pleasurable pursuits."

THE NEXT MORNING, after a night of uninterrupted sleep, Margaret noticed the light streaming through the windows. She went to stretch and felt something holding her down. She glanced over and saw Riverton. She couldn't remember lying down in his bed, but damn it all, she couldn't imagine a better way to wake up.

Then it hit her like a runaway coach—they were to be married this morning. For God's sake, he had told her that Tarleton had seen them in a compromising position, sleeping in the viscount's bed. How much more damning did it have to be?

She shook her head. Instead of moving James's arm to get out of bed, she poked him in the ribs to wake him gently. "James, we need to get out of bed or everyone will think that we are—"

Margaret stifled a cry when James pulled her into his arms and kissed her. Not just a peck but a passionate, bordering on bruising, kiss. He licked at her lower lip, as if asking for permission to enter. She opened her mouth and, God, that man could kiss. Warmth spread through her, filtering down deep into her belly.

She broke the kiss, pulling away. "We need to get dressed before Tarleton marches in through the door." She struggled not to touch him.

"I hate to say it, my dear, but you are too late for that. The bishop is here to preside over your vows. Now, get dressed and please, be presentable," Tarleton said from the door.

From beside her, James chuckled. She rolled her eyes. Men! She didn't know what to do with those in her life. Tarleton had turned into a matchmaker, and yet she was sure that he hadn't done whatever this was.

"We will be down soon. While you wait, can you go over to Ioan and Matilda's to see if they will be our witnesses?" Margaret asked her honorary uncle.

"We've already gotten that fixed. Once I told Matilda that

you were going to marry James, she wanted to provide the music. I suppose that she wants to play something special for you—to surprise your new husband with her musical acumen." The man dared to wink at her. She knew exactly what Matilda was planning on playing, and her lips lifted of their own accord into a smile.

Not long later, Margaret navigated the stairs in her best dress. It still wasn't up to the social standards of the *ton*, but it would do for what she was planning. She noticed Matilda sitting demurely at the pianoforte along the wall of the parlor where the staff had, thankfully, moved furniture so that people could stand. She couldn't believe how much the room had changed.

"Before we proceed, Her Grace would like to perform something along with the soon-to-be countess." Then Matilda mouthed the words that Margaret wanted to hear—she had found the music to the song by Robert Burns, "(Oh) My Love Is Like a Red, Red Rose." She couldn't help the giddy little girl inside her from rejoicing.

Margaret strode toward the piano. She turned and started singing, "My love is like a red, red rose that's newly sprung in June. My love is like a melody that sweetly plays in tune…"

She watched her audience as their jaws dropped open. Her sweet voice echoed through the room. She noticed that some of Riverton's staff had stopped what they were doing and stood fixated in the hall. Margaret didn't know if it was her voice or Matilda's piano playing. Either way, she relished the attention. She had missed this. Most of all, she had missed her friend.

Her eyes were fixed on the one person that she wanted to hear the song. Their lives would be forever changed, yet she knew in her heart that she loved James. He had stolen her heart—and maybe she had stolen his.

It was the truth in James's eyes that brought tears to hers. A dangerous blend of lust and desire simmered under the surface. She couldn't help but respond through her voice, singing just to him. It wasn't until moments later when the song ended that she surveyed the room.

Margaret strode over to where James was standing. The man pulled her close and whispered, "You are awe inspiring."

A blush stole over her face. "Thank you, my lord. Maybe you and I will sing next time." She winked at him.

"Shall we commence with the vows before someone else decides to play an instrument for the group?" the bishop asked.

Not a hand came up, thank God.

"Can we make this short and sweet, bishop?" Margaret said, shifting from one foot to another.

Before she knew it, she was saying her vows to James—and James said his to her—and then he kissed her with great passion. The clapping from the people in the room and the staff members still congregating in the hall startled her from the kiss.

JAMES HAD LITTLE patience for the wedding feast that Cook had prepared on short notice. He was randy and needed his bride, so much so that he could barely walk straight without someone noticing the rather inconvenient tent in his britches. Luckily, the fashion of the day allowed for such issues. He pulled at his waistcoat and adjusted his britches. He had to shake his head and roll his eyes at his own thoughts.

Margaret clutched his arm and pulled him down to her so that she could whisper in his ear.

"When can we leave?"

He couldn't help but laugh. His bride was a diamond, a precious jewel. "Now?"

James wasn't the least bit surprised when Margaret pulled him toward the stairs up to his rooms. She was just as desperate as he was. God! He had been running around with his cock at half-mast for weeks now. Of course, that didn't help with his leg, but he was fine with that. Maybe Margaret would help with his little—big—problem.

The giggles coming from the front hall echoed around the house as James fought to keep up with his bride, who was racing upstairs as if the fires of hell were licking at their heels.

"Maybe it is a love match," James heard someone say from below. "His parents were a love match, also."

Then he stumbled. His parents had died some time ago. James and his sister, Grace, were all that were left of his family. Grace had just turned eighteen a few weeks back and wanted a London Season. With James's job, he didn't think it would be something that she should do, nor something he wanted her to do. His sister and Silas Hutchinson had gotten along well, but he wasn't sure he wanted a former Shadow agent in the family. Edinburgh held a Season, and he would feel slightly better about having her attend the one closer to home.

Damn and blast, he yelled at himself. Grace wasn't here. He had promised his sister that he wouldn't marry without her being there. Unfortunately, since he was found with Margaret in a compromising position, the haste of the nuptials couldn't be helped. They would have to have a small party at Rosebriar House for those who were unable to make it to the wedding, which was more people than he wanted to admit.

He felt Margaret pull on his arm as they came to the big oak doors that marked his rooms. He picked her up and held her while she opened the doors from his arms. He walked her over the threshold of their rooms and carefully made his way to the bed.

"You don't have to carry me; I know your leg hurts from all the standing. Please..." Margaret said before he gently placed her on the bed.

"My leg doesn't hurt. I wanted to carry you; I wanted you in my arms. You are mine," he growled into her ear. He felt, as well as saw, the goosebumps on her arm and neck. He was acting possessive, and for the first time, it felt right to be. He wanted the best for her. He would protect her.

"And you are mine," Margaret chimed in.

James nodded and sat down on the edge of the bed. "You are beautiful, darling. Inside and out. I can't believe that we wasted so much time."

He lowered his face to hers and gently brushed a kiss upon her upturned lips. She was perfect for him. He felt her as she tried to get on her knees to get more of him. No. Their first time making love would be at his pace, even if he had to tie her hands to the four-poster bed to keep her from moving. Just the thought forced more blood to his cock. He couldn't believe how hard he was. Never had a woman affected him so much.

The kiss went from a gentle brushing of lips to a passion-driven feast in short time. James couldn't help but bite her lower lip to gain entrance into the warm haven of her mouth. Thank the Lord, she took his encouragement and opened to him. He deepened the kiss.

"We need to get you out of this gown," he said as he helped her to her knees on the bed and turned her so that her back was to him. He slowly unbuttoned the gown and slid the material from her shoulders, down her arms, and watched as it pooled around her waist. Even with her chemise and stays, he couldn't hold back his hum of approval.

"You are stunning," he whispered in her ear before he continued to kiss down her neck to the junction of her shoulder.

James could feel her heartbeat pick up speed. Dear Lord, he couldn't wait to have her, but he needed to make sure that she was ready for him. He was well endowed and didn't want to hurt her. He knew that she had been engaged before, so he wouldn't be shocked if she wasn't a virgin. He had lost his virginity some time ago to a milkmaid who had the largest breasts he had ever seen—and yet he almost wanted to go back in time to wait for his beautiful bride.

History was that—history. He couldn't change it, but he could make this evening the best he could make it. Hopefully his leg would be able to take the abuse for the next several hours. Yet he could have Margaret do some of the work. He smiled to himself as he kissed his way down to one of her breasts, pulled it from the confines of her stays, and took the nipple into his mouth.

The moan that came from Maggie spoke to him, letting him know that she enjoyed what he was doing to her. He lightly bit on the nipple and sucked it into his mouth for a moment before laving attention on the other breast. Desire rode him hard, wanting him to pound his cock into her soaked sheath, but she wasn't quite there yet.

MARGARET COULDN'T KEEP herself from moving, trying to get what she wanted. She couldn't think beyond the need trying to force its way out. She had, for a moment, forgotten where she was. James's tongue stroked her nipple, and she couldn't hold back. *"James!"*

"I want to hear your sounds. I want to hear you scream my name," he said as he traced a trail down her belly to the heart of her pleasure. She couldn't breathe.

In all her previous liaisons, Margaret had never been so stimulated, so out of her mind with pleasure. She shivered when she felt his tongue dip into her navel. She arched her back to take more, but James didn't do anything but make her want to take what she needed from him. Just as she was going to flip over, she realized that the man was still dressed.

"My lord, there seems to be a problem…"

"Oh? What is that, darling?" he replied. *How dare he.*

"You seem to be overdressed for our event." She giggled.

"You think so?"

Margaret stared at him as he slowly started to disrobe. The man was everything she wanted in a lover, even if she'd never thought she would marry. Best laid schemes and all. Yet she couldn't pull her eyes away from him. He was built like one of the Elgin Marbles, chiseled like a master sculptor's masterpiece. To her, he was the only thing coming between her and what she need now, and that was his co—

Her thoughts scrambled when James pulled down his britches and that part of him, his cock, jutted out from a thatch of blond hair. She followed the small path of hair up his torso to his face. This man was hers.

"Am I dressed for the occasion now?" James cocked an eyebrow.

"Yes," Margaret moaned in response.

She didn't know what would happen next, but James started right where he left off—just above her sex. Then he was there, and oh God, she held her breath as James licked the small nub between her legs. Margaret arched, wanting more, wanting release more than anything.

"Please, James, don't stop!" She moaned as he continued to torture that little nub with his tongue and teeth.

"I wasn't going to." He pulled away from her for a moment.

"I want more!" she sang as James put two fingers in her. She couldn't think—all she could do was feel as he continued to thrust his fingers into her.

Chapter Nine

J AMES COULDN'T BELIEVE that this was how his day was going to
end, with him claiming his wife, one torturous nibble at a time.
He glanced up at her as he dived back between her thighs and felt
her inner muscles quiver and shake as her climax came closer.
Her juices ran into his mouth as his fingers did the rest.

A keening call came from her as she came in his mouth.
Damn, that was something to behold. "I am going to take you
now. If you want me to stop, now is a good time." James needed
consent. He always had. He was an honorable rake, if there was
such a thing.

"Yes, I need you so badly," Margaret replied as he lined his
cock up to her entrance and thrust into her in a single shot.

He couldn't believe how good she felt as he continued to
thrust in and out of her, feeling her body embrace his cock. He
was on a tight leash, and he felt his balls tighten as the rush of
tingling up his spine let him know that this time—

By God, he couldn't hold back. He plucked and flicked at her
nub while his thrusts became more powerful.

"Come for me, love," he commanded as he felt her inner
muscles clench his cock like a glove, and it took him to the edge
of the cliff. His climax struck as hers began—and they went over
the cliff together.

Several moments later, James couldn't bring himself to move,
but he had to because he was sure that he was too heavy for

Margaret to be his pillow and mattress. He maneuvered them both toward the middle of the bed with Margaret's head resting on his shoulder. It had never dawned on him that he would make love to the woman that he had been head over heels with since he was a young lad. Fuck, he could barely think at all, so why was he thinking about when he was younger?

James glanced down at his wife and smiled. He had her in his arms, and he would never let go, in sickness or in health. He would be there to protect her. For now, though, a light rest would do his body good. He closed his eyes and fell asleep.

MARGARET WOKE TO a frightening sound coming from beside her. James was groaning in agony and nearly pushed her off the bed when he tossed and turned. What was wrong with him? She didn't know what to do. Call for the doctor across the street who happened to work with Uncle Anthony?

"Wake up, James. Please," she said, not knowing what was going on.

"I am so sorry, Benjamin. So sorry," James cried out in his sleep.

Margaret searched her memory for a Benjamin. Then it dawned on her—Benjamin Hartley had been James's friend and colleague during the wars. He had died in the Battle of Waterloo. She couldn't imagine the pain her husband had to go through to make it through alive—just to find out that his friend had perished several feet behind him.

She had saved every news clipping and sheet about the war to see if anyone she knew had been killed at the hands of the French. She had nothing against the Frenchmen as a people. No. What she had against them were the men that they had killed or could have killed. It was their fault that she was a spy. It was because of them that she saw the loss of life in the fields of Waterloo. She'd scoured those fields looking for a lost lordling that was supposed to be on his grand tour but ended up in the wrong place at the wrong time. She didn't find him.

She glanced back at her husband. What he was experiencing was nothing that she had ever seen before, but she had heard enough about it. She needed to wake him up. She went over to the chest of drawers not far from the bed that had a pitcher of water. No, she would not dump all the water on his face, but she planned on dipping her hand in the water and sprinkling some of the cool liquid over his face—hopefully waking him up.

She glanced at the clock and noticed the time. She didn't want to wake the staff, but she didn't know what else she could do— other than running across the street, but that was not an option for her. Someone needed to stay with James to make sure that he didn't hurt himself while he was dreaming.

She had heard stories of when soldiers came home from war, how they weren't themselves. She could imagine. Margaret hadn't been on the front lines; it wasn't her role in the war. But she had seen the carnage firsthand. She had nightmares months after returning home. It was because of those dreams that she returned to the old religion. Not Christianity. She had no need for that religion. It was the religion of her father. She was more into the old ways.

When Margaret was younger, her Irish mother started teaching her about the healing properties of certain plants. She was told the stories of the stars, and of the Celts of old that were powerful. Even now, she could remember her mother's voice teaching her about the old religion. She bent her head in meditation. She took a couple of deep breaths to calm herself and went about what she needed to do for James.

Margaret had heard that touch, sometimes, woke people out of dreams. Touch, it would seem, was a way to show love, and maybe—just maybe—hers would jolt him from the demons that chased him. She touched his face with both of her hands, nearly getting rolled over in the process. She held on, and slowly, James quieted down. She watched in disbelief as he turned on his side and started to softly snore.

She would need to contact the doctor later. She hoped that James hadn't hurt his leg during the ordeal.

Margaret crawled back on the bed, under the sheets, and prayed that he would be fine in the morning. She laid her head down on the pillow and felt her husband's arms wrap around her—and she drifted off into sleep.

Chapter Ten

LILY WOKE UP early in the morning to get ready for her day out in the wilds of London. She had spoken with her mother and father about the viscount's offer. Neither one wanted to accept charity, but with the offer of jobs, they couldn't refuse. That was why she was up so early, and she was regretting it. She needed to get to the viscount's house before she had to be at Saint George's.

She couldn't put a finger on what was different about the day. She couldn't help but wonder what would happen—and that scared her. The easy part was going to the viscount's house. The hard part was yet to come.

Lily quickly dressed in her serviceable gown and put her shoes on for a long day on her feet. She rushed out the door and then skidded across the cobblestones in front of her house when a large shadow emerged from behind one of the other houses. She tried to scream, but a gloved hand quieted her.

"Be quiet or I will use my knife to quiet you." The man put a sharp metal object at her throat. Lily couldn't keep him from hurting her unless she did what he said. In her mind, she went over every possible way to get out of the fix she was in. The only logical choice was to let the man take her and try to escape. She knew of a couple of options if he placed her in a carriage.

"You are coming with me. The Priest wants to speak with you, and I am to get you to him." The man spoke in a fine accent, not one from the rookeries.

Lily couldn't make out where she had heard the voice before, but she knew that she had, in fact, heard the man speak before. Maybe it was at the viscount's. She couldn't be sure.

She nodded. "I will go with you. Please, put away the knife."

As she asked, the man put down the knife. Her plans for the day had been forced in another direction. Her mind wandered to the missive that she had taken to the viscount's house the day before. It was still in Riverton's hands, thank God. Did the Priest know that she had taken the missive to the viscount? Did he have her followed?

JAMES WOKE AS the sun streamed through the windows. He felt well rested for the first time in a long time—since before he joined the dragoons. He pulled Margaret closer to him. Just as he nibbled on her ear, a knock came at the door.

"Come in," James said while rolling his eyes. His staff needed to learn not to interrupt him as he was trying to seduce his bride.

"My lord, a missive. The delivery boy said it was urgent," the footman said as he handed James a note.

He sat straight up when he read what the missive said. God-damn it all to hell and back. He had placed his best man at Lily's house, and the man was found murdered and the girl was gone. Fuck it all. He fumbled for his banyan and slippers before nearly tripping out of the bed. He wasn't that graceful on the best of days. Then it occurred to him that his leg wasn't working at all. What happened to his leg?

"George, I need you to go over to Tarleton's house and wake Elijah. I also need to you to go to the Duke of Rathdrum's house and have them come over as well," he commanded from the edge of the bed.

Usually the only time his leg would do something like this was when he had a nightmare. But he hadn't had a nightmare that he remembered. Normally, he remembered every single one. He would remember thrashing, and the bloody dreams would haunt him all day.

He glanced over at Margaret's sleeping form. In the dark hours of the early morning, he could've sworn that he felt her hands on his face.

He tapped lightly on Margaret's shoulder to wake her up. He needed to know what had happened to him to, because whatever this was made his leg feel like it could break at any moment.

"Love, it's time to wake up. I need to talk with you," he whispered in her ear. The moan that she emitted from her lips broke the spell that had him enthralled.

"Can't it wait till morning?" Margaret sleepily asked.

"It is morning, love. We need to get up. We are going to have guests here in a moment. There seems to be a bit of a problem. One, my leg isn't working, and I think you witnessed one of my spells. Two, your little friend is missing, and one of my best men was killed watching her house last night."

Margaret shot up, barely catching the blanket before it slid to the mattress. "You had a nightmare last night. I hoped that it wouldn't affect your leg, but I guess my hopes were in vain. Once my hands were on you, the dream subsided. What's this about Lily?"

"We really don't know right now until we can get Rathdrum here, and maybe even Tarleton. All we know is that Patrick had been watching the house. He was found facedown in the Thames just a couple of hours ago. I would hate to describe what the missive said about a second smile." James shook his head. He had seen many things during the wars, but he had never read such a description of someone being nearly decapitated by a butcher's knife.

"What happened to Lily? Does anyone know?"

"All we know is that she is missing. I think it might be because of the missive she didn't deliver as directed yesterday. I hope she can effect her own escape. She is a rather resourceful young lady from what you've told me and what I gleaned from what she told me about her life." James swept his fingers through his hair.

"I hope you're right, husband. I really hope you're right."

NONE THE WORSE for wear, Lily sauntered up to the viscount's house. Her hair was a mess, her clothes were beyond repair, and her shoes were missing. She couldn't help but wonder why she'd been abducted in the first place. She thought back on her ordeal. The man did have a carriage that she was put into. In fact, the dolt put her in the storage space under the seat, which was exactly where she'd wished he would put her.

She knew just the right angle for her to drop out of the space and onto the cobblestone roads without being seen. She wished that the man would've given her a little bit more excitement. That was easy. Too damn easy.

The hair on the back of her neck spiked up, and she swung her head from one direction to another. Lily couldn't see anyone, yet there were plenty of dark corners to hide in. The man who'd abducted her could have made it easy for a reason, and she hoped that she was wrong about that. She shook her head and knocked on the viscount's door.

The butler opened the door, took one look at her, and almost closed the door in her face.

"Let her in," came a voice that she barely recognized from behind the door.

The butler nodded and proceeded to guide her into the house. She felt horrible tracking dirt—or was it mud?—and all sorts of unimaginable things into the viscount's house. She stood in the hall, head down, when she heard shoes clomping from somewhere in the house. The sound echoed throughout the hall. She looked up to find Riverton standing in front of her.

"What happened? We heard you were abducted."

"I was on my way here when a man came out of the shadows and put his hand over my mouth. He spoke in a cultured accent. I never saw his face. I was smarter than him, though," Lily said. She didn't need to give specific information—the gist of the abduction was all she needed to give him, right?

Riverton nodded. "The same man managed to kill my best man, who had been watching your house. I would feel safer if you and your family came to live here."

Lily stood stoically. "I was going to tell you that they felt the same way. That's why I was out as early as I was."

She had been strong through the whole thing, but now she felt tears streaming down her face. Lily didn't normally cry in front of people, but she couldn't stop. She was safe. She had gotten herself free.

"There may be someone following me. I didn't see him, but the hairs on the back of my neck let me know that someone was watching," she said after the tears stopped.

"We will be watching. I have some men I can put as guards on the house for now. Until then, I will send someone over to get your parents and their belongings. Are you expected to make deliveries today?" Riverton asked.

Lily knew that she should, to keep her work with the Valor and Honor investigators a secret, but something inside her suggested that the man she delivered those missives for already knew. She shivered.

Riverton saw the shiver and changed topics.

"Let's get you a bath and a change of clothes. I don't think you are in any shape to go out. We don't want you catching cold." The viscount waved his arms to and fro for his servants to get a suite ready for her.

It had been a while since Lily had lived in the lap of luxury, with servants and peace. She sighed. She couldn't wait until she could dip into a hot bath, the extravagance of which she hadn't had in a long time. Ever since her father was injured and her brother died—and the mine on the estate had dried up. They'd had to sell the house and all their belongs just to make enough for the small house they had in one of the worst parts of London.

At that moment, Margaret came down the stairs in the hall. The woman was graceful and absolutely one of the most beautiful women of Lily's acquaintance.

"Lily!" Margaret raced down the last couple of stairs and wrapped her in a tight embrace.

Every emotion that Lily had held back threatened to crumble as she held on to her friend. Her coming to the viscount's house could put her friend in danger. She stepped out of the embrace.

"I may have led someone evil to your door. I wish I hadn't come here, but I didn't know anywhere safer." Lily sniffled.

"I think you may be correct in that assumption. We need a meeting, not just with Tarleton, but the Valor and Honor investigators too. And you will help us find who did this."

If there was anything that made her feel even safer, it was the mention of the Valor and Honor investigators. That gave her hope. She would help them help her. What she wanted, above all else, was the safety of her parents.

A footman brought her back from her inner thoughts. "Miss, your suite is ready and a bath is waiting. Please follow me."

Lily glanced up to see the man standing in front of her, motioning for her to follow him. She did as he bade and followed him up the stairs. When they got to the door, a maid stood sentry over the room. Lily noticed the slight nod from the maid to the footman, as if one was handing her off to the other. It was a wordless conversation between the two servants.

When she entered the room, Lily was in awe. She quietly and quickly disrobed and was helped into the bath. She sighed as the other woman went about her work to clean her from the top of her head down to the tips of her toes. She had missed this. She sighed and closed her eyes.

JAMES GLANCED OVER at Margaret. "We need to have a meeting here. I don't want Lily left alone until we can figure out what is going on and find a safe place for her and her parents."

"You're thinking of going up to Scotland?"

James nodded. "Since my sister is up there, with many guards, it may be the most logical place to have them. Grace is of the same age as Lily."

"It would be a great place for her, but I don't think it would be the best for her parents. Her mother is heavy with child and her father is still recuperating from his injuries. We need to send Robbie to have the others come here for a meeting, and we can discuss what is best once Lily is refreshed."

James knew that what his wife said was true. They had no time to spare if they were going to keep Lily from being harmed in the future. She was their proof that the Shadows existed, that their leader—the Priest—was real. Not that James had truly doubted their existence—he certainly fought against a secret society in a world of intrigue.

He had known his fair share of intelligence specialists, which he guessed would be safer to say than *spies*. They gathered information from all places: balls, fetes, the baths, and wherever else people gathered. Margaret had been such a person, but she also had another designation—assassin. If he hadn't known her before the death of her fiancé, he would be scared to be in the same room with her. Tarleton had suggested before that she was his best.

James didn't need to see her in action to know that she could kill a man with her bare hands. He glanced down at his wife, whose head was tilted up to his. He brought his hands up to cup her jaw, bent his head, and kissed her. She opened for him, and he slid his tongue into her mouth. She tasted of tea, strawberries—obviously from her breakfast—and the taste of her, the essence of her. He couldn't get enough of her.

He pulled back from her for a moment. "Love, we need to get the others here."

James had forgotten that his butler had been standing sentry by the front door. He glanced over at the man. "Has anyone sent for Lord Tarleton and Rathdrum's residences? If so, what's taking so long?"

"Yes, my lord. Do you want me to send the footman to Master Phineas's residence, as well?"

"Of course, yes. We will need him."

James knew that there was nothing that would hinder him from finding out who'd abducted his new charge and what happened to Bryan Jeffers. In his mind, he knew that when he figured out one, he would ultimately figure out the other. It sounded like something that Jeffers would do. The man was ruthless. Just months ago, he had killed an accomplice in cold blood, in front of James and his friends.

Jeffers was dangerous. But James had a feeling that they had yet to find out how dangerous the man really was.

Chapter Eleven

MARGARET CLIMBED THE stairs to check on Lily. James had gone into his study to wait for the investigators and Tarleton to show up. She, on the other hand, wanted to make sure that Lily wasn't suffering any injuries with what happened to her earlier. Margaret knew that Lily was strong, much stronger than anyone gave her credit for.

She stopped at the door to Lily's suite and knocked. Margaret barely heard the soft "enter" before she turned the doorknob and entered the spacious room. The gown that she had given Lily to wear looked exquisite on her. It highlighted the woman's natural curves and brought out her lavender eyes. Lily's hair was in a beautiful plait with tendrils of curls framing her face. If only her parents were here to see her.

"You are beautiful, Lily!" Margaret couldn't hold back the need to encourage the younger woman.

"The dress is—"

"You can keep it. I have a feeling you may need it soon." Margaret winked.

A short knock on the door broke their conversation. Margaret eyed the door as she strode over and opened it. "Elijah, what are you doing here?"

"I heard that someone may need my…"

The look on the man's face was one of shock and surprise. Margaret couldn't help but giggle. The doctor's jaw had dropped.

He clearly appreciated the beautiful woman in the room.

"Lily, I didn't know it was you who… I don't know what I'm trying to say, but you're beautiful," Elijah stammered.

Margaret watched as the two other occupants of the room stared at each other. It was so intimate that she thought of leaving the room, but that would leave Lily unchaperoned. She had to laugh at fate. She had forgotten that Elijah was the doctor in charge of Lily's mother during her current pregnancy.

"Elijah, we need to make sure that she is unharmed. She promised me that she wasn't hurt, but we thought that she might want to see a doctor nonetheless."

He nodded. "Of course. If you would stay in the room, since you are a married woman now, you can chaperone. I won't do a full examination, but I will check for broken bones and bruising. I can already see her hands are injured from a fall?"

"I fell out of a carriage." Lily blushed.

"I fear there is more to that story, doctor, but for now that will have to suffice," Margaret added.

She continued to watch as the doctor examined Lily, making sure there were no broken bones or serious cuts or scratches. The bruises would heal within a couple days. Her friend's left wrist was bright green, indicating a possible break. It could have been much worse—Lily could still be at the mercy of her abductor.

Something inside Margaret told her that the worst had yet to come. That something was lurking in the shadows. That someone wanted Lily dead or unable to talk about her delivering missives for a man. Ultimately, she knew that Lily was keeping something from her. Something potentially harmful to her husband and his friends.

JAMES WAS SITTING in the chair behind his desk when Ioan and Phineas strolled into the study. The two men were as close as brothers to him, since he didn't have a brother and his only sister was living in Scotland. Behind them, Tarleton leaned against the door, arms crossed.

"What is the meaning of this meeting?" Tarleton asked, clearly annoyed.

"The young woman you met here not too long ago was abducted early this morning. She somehow managed to escape and found her way back here. She mentioned that someone had followed her but stayed in the shadows." James stood from behind his desk.

"Why do we need to be here?" Ioan demanded.

"As Tarleton knows, Lily has been delivering some missives for a man out of Saint George's. We think the man may be the Priest."

James eyed Ioan as the situation dawned on him. "Does she know who he is?" he asked.

"She hasn't indicated that she does, but I know she is holding something back. Something she may be scared to say. I do not think she is a threat to us, but I do think that you need to meet her first to find out for yourselves." James tugged on the bellpull and waited for a footman.

"My lord?"

"Please bring my wife and Miss Lily to me," James responded.

The footman bowed and exited the room.

Moments later, the ladies joined them in the study. The room was large, but not nearly large enough for the people now standing in it. James was tempted to move the group to the parlor or even the music room.

"She looks familiar." Phineas seemed fascinated with Lily.

"Her father fought beside me, Colonel Thompson."

Phineas tilted his head and hummed. "I see a small resemblance. Why does she look like she went five rounds with an underground pugilist?"

"I escaped through the bottom of a carriage after being abducted by a man I don't know," Lily exclaimed. "I don't want to talk about my experiences this morning, but I see that I don't have much choice."

James nearly applauded her. He could tell the young woman was done talking. He smiled when Elijah entered the room, and watched as the doctor tried to keep his emotions under control.

"My patient should be in bed resting. Why is she down here?" Elijah asked.

James glanced at Tarleton, who was also smiling at the commotion in the room. He marched over.

"I don't see your being the culprit, but the smile on your face reminds me of the cat who stole the cream. You had the same look on your face when you barged into my rooms and demanded I marry Margaret." James kept his voice quiet.

"I had nothing to do what with happened to Lily or you or Margaret. I just used my power to persuade you to act on your own feelings. I did nothing more than that. If you didn't want to marry Margaret, you didn't have to—but you wanted to."

James sneered at the spymaster.

"Now, none of that," Tarleton continued. "Margaret is like a niece to me. I knew her family. When they disowned her, I took the place of guardian. She needed someone to stand up for her. Luckily for her, I also knew of her talent with a pistol, knives, and rope. I gave her purpose, and it saved her life."

James had known some of what the spymaster said was true. There wasn't much that he could do about Margaret's past, but he knew that she did what she did because she was ordered to. There was still much he didn't know about his wife, and eventually, they would talk about her past. Until then, James would be patient.

"I see you understand what I've been trying to say all along," Tarleton said. "I trust Margaret and her instincts, but with Jeffers on the loose, we should move the women to Scotland. It would be easier to keep them safe. Your house there would be easier to defend if Jeffers were to infiltrate the house. London is too busy."

"Margaret and I have talked about sending Lily to the Highlands. It's going to be harder for her parents to join, for obvious reasons," James replied.

"Yes, but Margaret isn't a weapon that I would use in an enclosed area such as Mayfair. It's too busy. Out in the moors of Scotland, she could easily hide and…"

From the corner of the room, James noticed his wife staring at him. She didn't seem happy about something, and he figured it was the current topic. He watched as Margaret took Lily's hand and dragged her through the people and out into the hall.

James didn't know what was wrong until he caught a whiff of something not right. Then it dawned on him—smoke was wafting in from under the door leading to the conservatory.

"Everyone outside, now!" he shouted.

As James and his friends made it out of the study, the servants were already extinguishing the flames. "What happened?" James asked a footman who had a bucket of water in his hands.

"I'm not sure, my lord. Initially, something was thrown in through the window." The footman pointed to a broken windowpane in the door.

"I see, but I fail to understand how that started a fire."

"Well, Cook had all of us making sure everything was put away for the night, and one of the maids had been told to make sure everything was locked up tight," the footman said. "She was here when the item was thrown through the window, and she dropped the candle she was holding, my lord. She didn't mean to."

"She is not in trouble; I guarantee you that. I don't blame her for the damage to my home and will not be making her pay for what happened. I do need to speak with her about what occurred, though." James knew that the maid felt it was her fault that the hall and part of the parlor needed to be repaired. He was lucky that his staff loved the house as much as he did.

The footman looked around him, seeing that the fire had been put out. "She is my sister, my lord. I will get her for you."

"That is not necessary for now. Thank you. Please put that

bucket away, and we will speak of this again later. In the meantime, can you tell me where the item is that broke my window?" James asked.

The footman pointed to the brick on the floor near the door. James bent over and picked it up. On the back side a message read, bright as day, *Give us Lily, or you will pay!*

"Ioan! We need to move the ladies north!" he bellowed. The protector in him screamed. He couldn't put the lives of all he knew in danger. He needed to get Margaret to safety. The logic of his fears didn't add up, but he needed to protect Margaret and her friend—and Ioan's little pixie, Matilda. Fuck!

"What is going on here, James?" Ioan asked from somewhere behind him.

"Come see for yourself," James replied, waving Ioan to him.

An audible gasp came from his friend. "I agree. I think we should all go to Rosebriar House, not Rathdrum Hall. Spreading out between three different homes is not conducive to keeping our women safe. We need to make sure that Gracie has better protection, as well."

James knew that his baby sister was part of the family he and his friends made. But to hear that his best friend wanted to protect her as much as the wives of the brotherhood... He just couldn't imagine a world without any of them.

Chapter Twelve

M ARGARET HEARD JAMES bellow something but couldn't make it out through the closed door. Apparently, the servants had put out the flames almost as soon as she caught the scent of something burning. She didn't know what had started the fire, but it had her husband upset.

Standing outside the house, she turned her back to the door and assessed the street. There were plenty of places to hide in the dark shadows.

Maybe Lily was right. Maybe someone was watching her. The sense of someone watching her caused the hairs on the back of Margaret's neck stick up. Where was the man—or woman? Given that she was an assassin, the Shadows may have a contracted assassin who was a woman too.

She surveyed the buildings around her, every garden and marble statue in the yards, and every window. Unless the Shadow agent owned or rented one of these grand houses, there was absolutely no way that he could make it into one of the build-ings—or could he?

Margaret remembered Matilda once saying that her uncle's house, the safe house, and the duke's residence had secret passageways throughout. Could there be underground tunnels from one house to another? She would have to ask Matilda if she had ever found one.

The door behind her snicked open, and her husband's warm

arms wrapped around her. She stiffened for a moment.

"What's wrong?" he asked as he kissed her neck below her ear. The man knew her buttons, and that was a big one.

"We are being watched. I can't figure out where they are hiding, but I know they are there. Lily was right—not that I didn't believe her before."

"Are you certain?" James asked in a whisper as he continued to kiss a path down her neck.

Margaret could barely hold back a moan of pleasure before responding, "Yes, of course I am. You know that feeling you get when you are being followed? I felt that, and my instincts are rather good."

James lifted his head and stared into her eyes. "I believe you. I've felt the same way since Lily found her way to our house. I don't know what is going on, but we need to tell Tarleton. In the meantime, I want to make love to my wife."

Margaret wholeheartedly agreed. She needed only what he could give her.

Margaret felt her feet leave the ground as James picked her up and strode back into the house. He carried her up the stairs to their rooms and deposited her onto the bed.

"Please..." she begged before James took his time worshipping her body.

FROM A SECRET room adjoining the viscount's chambers, a man dressed all in black waited. The last thing he'd ever wanted was to listen to Riverton make love to his wife. Damn the man he worked for—damn him to hell and back. Voyeurism wasn't something he was into. He shook his head. No matter what, he would have to wait until both participants fell asleep before he could do what he was sent to do.

He glanced down at the missive in his hand. He didn't know

what was in it, but that wasn't his job. His job was to deliver it, unnoticed, and leave the grounds immediately. Thank God he had lived in the townhouse down the street as a young boy and knew that there were tunnels between many of the houses.

Now that he knew that the safe house and the Duke of Rathdrum's house were connected—possibly in the same network of tunnels and passageways as the house he grew up in—he would need to let the man who hired him know. A wicked smile crossed his face. In the darkness of the room, he thought through his plan, the one given to him by another man with whom he worked on occasion.

The sounds from the other room died down. *Finally!* The viscount sure had stamina. He shook his head. He had work to do.

He pushed on the hidden door in the wall and quietly maneuvered around furniture and discarded clothing toward the bed where the two lovebirds lay in each other's arms. His heart skipped a beat at the sight, but he continued with his purpose. He carefully laid the missive against the small clock on the stand next to the bed before escaping the room.

THE NEXT MORNING came too soon for James. He had dealings at his office to do, and he wasn't looking forward to the time away from Margaret. He felt around the stand next to the bed and felt something that wasn't supposed to be there—a missive. He never placed stationery near candles, even if the candle wasn't lit. Which reminded him of the fire—was it just a day ago? Everything in this house was flammable, from the art to the rugs to the library. He didn't know where the missive came from, but he would have to analyze it soon as he could.

James sat up in the bed, bent over to place a sweet kiss on Margaret's temple, and whispered that he was going to his study.

He pushed himself to get out of bed, pulled on his banyan, and strode with purpose to his study, the missive in hand.

"My lord, would you like your morning tea brought here?" his valet asked from the doorway, carrying the clothing he would wear for the day.

"Please. I received this missive sometime last night while I was sleeping. It was on the stand next to my bed. You wouldn't know anything about that, would you?" James asked.

"No, my lord. Would you like me to speak to the rest of the staff?" the valet asked.

"I don't think that is necessary. I will figure it out, eventually. Now, if you would please bring me tea, I can get to this pressing matter in my hand." James waved the stationery in his hand and laughed when the valet's lips formed a smile.

James placed the missive on his desk, pulled the sides apart, and opened it. He glanced down and noticed the coded words in the message. As he was ready to pull his cipher out of a hidden drawer in his desk, a knock came at the door, and a maid came into the study carrying a tray with steeping tea and some pastries that Cook had baked earlier in the morning.

"Thank you." James always liked to thank his staff. Sure, they were servants, but his house wouldn't run as efficiently without them—and he wouldn't be alive without them.

The maid blushed. "You're welcome, my lord."

He waited for the maid to leave, grabbed the cipher, and went to work decoding the letter. What seemed like just a moment later, the snick of the door let him know that someone had joined him. Looking up, James noticed Margaret sauntering toward him. He couldn't take his eyes from her.

"What has you awake so early?" Margaret asked as she sat in one a chair on the other side of his desk.

"I found this missive on the stand next to the bed, by the candle."

James's eyes dropped back to the letter, and he kept decoding it. He felt unsure of why he didn't want Margaret in his office, reading the missive over his shoulder. She was his partner, not just in life but in this business with Tarleton. He searched out the clock standing on the mantel. He would have to take back his thought—it wasn't business hours yet. It had still not reached six o'clock in the morning. James sighed.

"Darling, I need to decode this missive first and then we can do as we please." James raised his eyes to hers. He knew in that instant that Margaret understood him.

"Can I help, or do you need Matilda?"

"I almost have this decoded, and then I can take it to Tarleton or Rathdrum," he replied with the quill in his grasp.

Just moments later, the message was laid out in front of him. James knew that both of his superiors needed to see what he had been working on. He noticed that Margaret hadn't moved from where she stood several moments before. He picked up the deciphered missive.

"Let's give this to Rathdrum, and then, my lovely bride, I want to make love to you." The twinkle in James's eyes shone brightly.

"It's only six o'clock, love," she said. "If you are going to be able to go into the shipping office and do what you are doing now, you need some rest."

He couldn't agree more. His eyes were barely open, and the soft glow of the candles was causing his eyes to ache. Maybe with the sun shining in through the windows, he would be able to focus better in a couple of hours.

Margaret held out her hand to help him out of his chair and lead him back up the stairs to their rooms.

✦

Chapter Thirteen

SEVERAL DAYS AFTER she was abducted, Lily was standing outside the door to her parents' house helping them move their meager belongings into one of Riverton's coaches. The viscount had offered to send several of his servants to help her, since her parents weren't able to do any of the heavy lifting.

It didn't take long for them to get back to Riverton House. A couple of the footmen helped bring her father into the house and up the stairs to their new lodgings. They were to stay as guests because of her father's rank. This was not at all shocking for Lily, and she loved that Riverton would treat her family as equals, despite how far they had fallen.

Neither she nor her parents wanted pity. Pity did none of them any good. It had been her self-pity that put her in the clutches of whoever hired her. Never again. She would never again go to such lengths to assuage her guilt.

As Lily stopped chastising herself, Elijah strode up to her. She had been having dreams about him, and she blushed. Some of them were erotic in nature, and there was no way she could feel comfortable around the doctor now.

"How are my patients today?" Elijah asked.

Lily looked into his beautiful eyes, searching for who knew what. "Both of my parents are in their rooms, thankful for the wonderful treatment by the viscount. Would you like me to take you to them?"

The doctor shook his head. "That isn't necessary. Riverton told me which suite was theirs. I wanted to visit with you, if I may?"

Lily stood in shock. Was she dreaming? Why would such a man want to visit with her? "Shall we go to the parlor, then?" she asked.

Elijah nodded. He spoke few words, but those he did speak were profound. She was on tenterhooks to find out what he wanted from her. She guided him to the parlor and sat in one of the chairs near the windows. Not for a moment did she think of having a chaperone—it didn't even faze her. The doctor was a man of honor and didn't want her in that way.

Still standing, Lily waited for Elijah to sit, but he did not. He paced back and forth on the viscount's priceless rug.

"What's the matter, my lord?" she asked.

"You are in trouble, my dear. I know, I know. Your life is at stake, and I don't like it one bit…"

What? Lily waited for him to elaborate.

"We don't know each other very well, but I feel protective of you. I want to be the one who looks after you and tends to you when you need it. I want to be the one you come to when you need someone to talk to, or to embrace you when you need to feel arms wrapped around you," Elijah continued. "I have been your friend through everything with your father's injuries and your mother's pregnancy. I want to be there for much, much more. I feel a connection with you, darling Lily. Please say that you feel the same?"

Lily stared at him. The look on her face, she assumed, was that of a fish in the nearby pool—mouth wide open in disbelief. Was the doctor going to propose? She searched her thoughts. She couldn't deny that there was something between them, yet neither had taken the step to further their relationship. Elijah was opening his heart to her, letting her know what he was feeling, what he wanted.

"Have we really been friends? I was working all the time

when you would come over to help my father and mother. Though, I'm glad you did. Oh, what am I saying?" Lily racked her brain for the words she needed to say. "We need to know each other better first…"

"I agree, but I-I want to find out what there is between us. I want to embrace this spark that flares every time we are close."

Lily felt that very same flare throughout her whole body when Elijah would enter a room. The air would sizzle with it.

"I want that too." Lily pushed herself off the chair and strode toward him. As she stood in front of him, she raised her hands to his face, cupped his jaw, and lightly caressed his cheek with her thumb. The hint of stubble shocked her—he was normally clean-shaven—but it suited him.

"May I kiss you?" Elijah asked as she stared up at him, never taking her eyes from his.

Lily had never been one to be brazen, never felt the embrace of a lover, yet she wanted to know Elijah in the most basic of ways. She wanted his arms around her, touching her, loving her. She pulled his head down and replied, "Yes, my lord," just as their lips met in a passionate kiss.

⇶✶⇷

NOT TOO FAR from Riverton House, a man lurked in the shadows. He smirked as he watched the couple kiss through the window. He was tasked with bringing her back to Saint George's for a meeting with the Priest. The man had hired him again. First, place a letter in Viscount Riverton's room. Second, continue to watch Riverton House.

The girl didn't deserve any of this. He knew, firsthand, what the Priest did to those who double-crossed him. They were never found, probably dropped into the Thames with weights. The same would happen to him if he didn't do what he had promised to do.

He was a peer of the realm, someone who had grown up with the men around him. He had gone to school with them, drunk with them, and gambled with them. He was trustworthy and honorable—or, at least, he once was. Now, he was a double agent working for two opposing spy networks. He was the reclusive gentleman, whispered about in ballrooms and written about in White's betting book. He was Edmund Alexander, the new Marquess of Grantham.

He hadn't gone by his given name in years. Edmund was a lifetime ago. Only a few people would recognize him, and even fewer knew him by name.

He continued to watch as the occupants of the parlor broke their kiss and looked into each other's eyes. Maybe one day, that would be him.

Chapter Fourteen

THE NEXT MORNING, James and Margaret sat at the breakfast table with the Duke and Duchess of Dunsbury. The Rakes, a hereditary spy network, were also investigating the deaths of Rathdrum's family. Since Ioan's family were bookkeepers for the Crown and had been on loan to the Rakes, they were an instrumental asset in the investigation. Apparently, Rathdrum's family weren't the only ones who were murdered. Most of the "Old Rakes" had been assassinated in "accidents" as well.

Margaret had worked with Her Grace many times in the past, as an agent, and for special events. She enjoyed the other woman's company and loved Juliana like a sister. The duke, on the other hand, was intimidating. His gaze never settled unless he was looking at his wife, and then his demeanor thawed for a moment before frosting over again.

"What have you found out?" Marcus, the duke, asked.

"Based on the coded notes in the library, they have linked the missing lordling to the Shadows and the Order. It's almost as if the two organizations are the same thing. Is it possible that it is true?" James replied.

Margaret glanced back and forth before adding her tuppence. "I don't believe so. The Order is much more regimented, while the Shadows are more ruthless."

Juliana, the duchess, spoke up. "I don't think that's true. The Order is ruthless in their pursuit of our people. They will go to any length."

Margaret nodded. She could think of a couple of times when she had come against some Order agents and nearly died in the process. The Shadows were killers, not just spies. That was not to say that the Order didn't hire assassins, because they did. They might be working together, but they weren't the same network.

"Are we sure? We haven't interrogated anyone from either network. They always poison themselves before we can, or they go underground," the duke said.

"I agree," James said. "Yet they seem to have the same goal. Whether they are different networks or not, they are trying to kill our members, and we need to apprehend them as soon as possible." He pounded on the table, and dishes clattered from the impact.

"All we know is that the former Duke of Rathdrum was looking into a young man who was fighting at Waterloo and disappeared not long after the battle. He is, supposedly, the only heir to a marquisate. The old marquis is ill and possibly on his deathbed—and the young man is still missing." Margaret watched as the men's minds churned toward the truth that she spoke.

"From what I gather, Tarleton has already been to the Continent to search for him there, and has since dispersed men to find him. Could the young man be dead?" the duchess asked.

The more Margaret thought on the matter, the more she believed the young man was a figment of someone's imagination. Yet, on the other hand, the notes left by the late Duke of Rathdrum held the possibility of finding the boy. She searched her memory. The man came from a family not far from where she lived as a girl.

"What are you thinking about, darling?" James asked from his spot at the head of the table.

"I remember this young man... He was the eldest son of a neighboring family. I don't recall his name, but there was some talk that he was the heir to a wealthy peer. I don't know what happened to him, but he may be the 'young man' we are trying to find. Though I wouldn't call him *young*. He was about my age."

All eyes seemed to focus on her. "I thought we were looking for a younger man?" James asked.

"If you call a man who just passed his majority as young, then yes. But he looked even younger than his years when I knew of him."

"What do you remember about his family?" the duke asked.

"They weren't titled, but they were well-to-do. They were gentleman farmers. I just don't remember a name. I would ask my family, but I'm not welcome to visit them. All we've got is Rathdrum's records and what the Crown may have on them."

Margaret burned with the need to solve this mystery. Maybe the church had records? Wasn't she advised by Tarleton to not go near the church? That had her laughing inside. A pagan going into a church—she couldn't help but wonder if lightning would strike her dead after she touched the door. Well, there was one way to find out.

"I am going to find out what the church has on them. I may have to go up to the Lake District, where my family is from, to find any information. What is the man's name?"

The Duke of Dunsbury glanced at her and nodded. "His name is Edmund Alexander."

⤜⟫⟫⟩⟨⟨⟪⤛

THE PRIEST SAT behind his desk, his cohort standing next to him. "We need to get the girl. She knows too much!"

"I had her, but she knew the weakness in the carriage. I should have prepared for that, but I didn't. For that, I apologize." The man combed his fingers through his limp hair.

The Priest knew that he couldn't trust even his own brother to do away with a loose end. *Damn and blast.* He would have to do it himself. He had hired Lily because she was tiny and could pass as a boy, but she grew a conscience. He couldn't wait to have her in his clutches. The problem was, he had promised his brother that he could take care of the Valor and Honor investigators—one at a time.

Bloodlust was something he would never understand, but loyalty was something that he prized in those he hired, and they would kill—if necessary. He glanced at the man beside him. "Our new man may be of use to you. He has already made his way into Riverton House and snuck into the viscount's rooms. It would be an easy feat to abduct the wench."

His brother grinned. "I look forward to killing her, slowly."

The Priest shuddered. The smile that crossed his brother's face was pure evil. He was beyond what the Priest would say was evil. The bastard was his worst nightmare come to life. The Priest was glad the man was on his roster and not the other side. He would regret the inevitable day that his brother would betray him.

A knock on the door pushed him out of his mind. "Come in!"

"You asked to speak with me." Edmund Alexander bowed.

"Yes. We have a chore for you. A young lady, living at Riverton House, has betrayed us. We need you to bring her in for questioning," the Priest commanded.

EDMUND COULDN'T BELIEVE what he was hearing. A young woman? There was a line he never crossed—no women or children, ever! He would have to speak with Tarleton, though he hadn't had contact with the man in an age. He couldn't risk himself being compromised. *Damn and blast.* He couldn't do this, yet he had no choice.

"Where am I supposed to bring this girl?" Edmund asked.

The Priest stared at him with his dark gaze. "Bring her to the country house. My friend here needs his privacy to do what he does best."

Something about the way the Priest spoke made Edmund shudder. He couldn't stop shivering at the thought that someone may die because of whom he worked for. *Fuck!* "I'm assuming you want me to proceed tonight?"

"Of course I do. Why would I ask you to do something this important if I didn't mean for it to happen today?" the Priest bellowed in response.

Edmund shuffled back toward the door. The man had a blazing temper that went with his auburn hair. The damn Scot was stubborn, and Edmund wanted to leave. But he needed more information to pass on. He needed the location of the country house before embarking on this dangerous mission.

"Will you give me the directions to the country house?" he asked, cringing with the effort it took him to force the words out.

The Priest stood from his chair. "You will take one of our carriages. I can guarantee that the conveyance has since been refurbished to keep the young lady inside. There will be no escaping this time! In addition, the driver will know where to take you once the deed is done."

Something about this whole mission seemed off to Edmund. This wasn't just an abduction and possible murder—this was revenge. For what? He didn't have time to think about that before the Priest sidled up next to him and pushed.

"It's time for you to go. You have a job to do. Now, go!" The man pushed Edmund straight out the door.

As Margaret tried to read through the missives and notes that the late Duke of Rathdrum had left behind, she had a thought. The name Edmund kept popping up in his notes. Could it be? She needed to have access to the Rathdrum records. She bolted from the chair she had been sitting in before righting the stacks of paper on her desk.

She pulled three times on the bellpull, and a footman knocked on the door moments later. "Ready a carriage, please. I need to go to Rathdrum House."

The footman nodded and sped down the hall to do what she had asked. Margaret pulled the bellpull again to signal for her lady's maid. She needed to get ready for her adventure into the Rathdrum records. She had never seen them before. The Dukes of Rathdrum held the most extensive records of births, deaths, and family in the British Isles—and some of the royal families throughout the Continent. They had been tasked with the knowledge and were trusted to keep those records safe.

Margaret grabbed her reticule from where she'd left it, which reminded her that she needed to clean her desk—at some point—and strode toward the front door to await the carriage. As she waited, the butler stood next to her.

"I will let my lord know that you are going to Rathdrum House." The butler pivoted to go back into the depths of the house when the carriage pulled onto the drive.

The ride to Rathdrum House took no more than fifteen minutes, but in Margaret's mind, it seemed like hours. She was staring out the windows of the carriage as the duke's house came into view. She was not expecting another carriage to be at the same place. Well, that may have put a stop to her research.

Then she saw the crest. Tarleton? What was he doing here?

The carriage came to a stop. The driver stepped down from his perch to open the door for her.

"Shall I stay here, my lady?" he asked.

"I don't think so. I will just ask Lord Tarleton to take me home when I'm done," she replied.

The driver nodded as he helped her alight from the carriage and get up the stairs to the entrance to the massive townhouse.

Margaret knew when the driver left her that she couldn't help the urge to open the door herself. She turned her head, searching the street. The hair on the back of her neck stood up. She surveyed her surroundings again and saw nothing. She searched the street, the windows of the houses around her. Nothing. Either her instincts were wrong or they were very correct.

As she stood, facing the door again, the Rathdrums' butler opened it and invited her in.

"His Grace and Lord Tarleton are in the library, in the records gallery. Would you like some refreshments?"

Margaret smiled. "Yes, please. I would like a tea tray brought in. I have quite a lot of research to do today. Oh, and some of your cook's best pastries wouldn't go amiss."

The butler announced her and turned on his heels to have a staff member bring her tea tray to the gallery.

Margaret strode through the room and found Tarleton and Rathdrum sitting at a circular table in an alcove of the library.

"Margaret, I didn't know you were going to be here today," Tarleton said, and he and Rathdrum stood as she approached.

"I remembered something from when I was young about a neighboring family and would like to view your family's records. And...I need to speak with both of you sometime today."

"What family do you want to view?" Rathdrum asked as he strode toward the gallery.

"The Alexander family."

She glanced up at Tarleton as she said the name. The spymaster was normally unshakeable, but this time, the look in his eyes was one of shock.

"What do you need to know about the Alexander family?" he probed.

"There are too many coincidences. The name Edmund was mentioned many times in the notes that the former Duke of Rathdrum left before his untimely death. There was a family that lived nearby my family's estate with a son named Edmund Alexander. They lived on an estate owned by a marquis, supposedly a relation of Edmund's father. There are more coincidences, but those are the ones I'm seeking answers to."

The glances between Tarleton and Rathdrum signified to her that they knew what she was going to research and aimed to stop her from doing so. She would go to Whitehall if need be to get the information. She knew the secretaries of each section within the government.

"I would rather you not look into this further, my lady," Tarleton said.

"Why? Because you know that I'm right? That he is the missing man that you have been looking for? I don't like secrets, Anthony," she pointed out. Secrets had gotten between her and her family. Secrets had killed her fiancé. Secrets had nearly destroyed her.

"Very well. Edmund Alexander is the new owner of that estate that you remember. He is also one of my best agents. With that being said, he has gone rogue. I haven't heard from him since Waterloo. The last I heard, he was on the Continent and received medical attention for wounds received in battle. Then nothing. Not one word," Tarleton recounted.

"How much does he know about the safe houses and the records?" she asked.

"He is privy to everything. He has had access, in the past, to the Rathdrum family records and knows the tunnel system under the houses on this block." The man stared into her eyes.

"Could he be back in London?"

"He could be…"

A footman entered the library with a small silver tray, indicating a message.

"My lord, a young messenger was asked to deliver you this." The footman handed the missive to Tarleton.

Margaret and Rathdrum watched as Tarleton opened the message and read it. She never understood how the spymaster could read something without showing emotion.

"The silence has been broken. It seems that our man is a double agent and has knowledge of another abduction attempt, later today. Rathdrum, if you could get the message out to your men that we will be removing ourselves from London and need to have armed guards for Lily Thompson and our good doctor, I would be grateful. Margaret, we need to get word to Riverton to procure a boat on short notice. Maybe he has one at the ready."

Margaret nodded. "I sent my carriage back to Riverton House. Will you be able to take me down to the docks? Riverton is at the shipping offices today."

"My carriage is at your disposal. I will stay here to manage things. Please, be careful. If my instincts are correct, this game is going to be deadly, and I want you to be at your best if things go as I think they will."

She knew that this was the spymaster speaking. The friend that she considered more of an uncle had been replaced. This man she trusted, but she knew her worries would be etched on her face. "I will be as safe as I can be. I have my blade with me, and some other weapons that I never leave home without. I should leave."

Tarleton lifted her hand and kissed it. "Send a messenger when you have a boat available for transporting at least fifteen people."

She nodded and marched toward the door. She was on a mission, and her body thrummed with excitement. This was what she lived for. The danger, the excitement, and all the possibilities.

Chapter Fifteen

JAMES SAT BEHIND his desk at the shipping company offices, scowling at the books of numbers. His company had been doing well, and exports and imports were at an all-time high. His accounts equaled out—as they should. Even knowing that all was apparently well, there was something that seemed off to him. The feeling of apprehension overshadowed everything.

He'd had the feeling once before, last year when the Rathdrum estate butler had been outed as a spy. The same man had escaped custody when his ship went down rounding the Horn of Africa and could very well be in London, hunting him. There was also the attempted abduction of Lily. The young woman had described the man, and the description reminded him of Jeffers.

Margaret, his beautiful wife, was at home with Lily—or he hoped she was. He needed to keep them safe, and the best place for that was his Highland estate where his sister resided. He could only imagine the mischief the women would get up to—add Matilda to the mix, and maybe Amelia, and he couldn't hold back his laughter.

Then it occurred to him that it would be safer and faster to take one of his ships. The *Endeavor*, his fastest and sleekest ship, was ready and could accommodate quite a few people. It was already prepared for a short journey and had enough food to feed all onboard. He wrote a short note for the captain of the vessel.

"Matthew!" he bellowed, hoping that the man was at his desk.

"Yes, my lord?"

"Walk this missive down to the *Endeavor* and see that it is delivered into the hands of the captain. No one else," James commanded.

Matthew, his man of all work, took the note from his hand. He bowed his head and exited the room. Knowing that his family and friends would be safe, James felt the weight lift from his shoulders for a moment. He looked at the ledgers and went back to work.

The squeak of the door opening broke his concentration. James looked up and found his wife standing in front of his desk. He took his pocket watch from where it lay and flipped it open. It wasn't time to go home yet. By the look on her face, something was wrong.

"Why am I blessed with your presence so early?" he asked.

"I'm here at Tarleton's request. Do you have a ship ready to leave port soon?"

James had known this would happen and was, once again, happy that he had made the *Endeavor* ready for travel—with guests. The ship was made for cargo, not for transporting passengers, but it would have to do.

"The *Endeavor* is already prepared for such a journey," he replied. "I'm sure that Tarleton and the rest will be here in moments. They should know that I keep one of my ships back, in case of situations like this."

James pulled himself from his chair and walked over to Margaret. He had missed her today. He'd missed her presence and her insight. He pulled her into his arms. She cuddled into him, and he held her close. He smelled her scent, which calmed him minutely. He dropped a kiss to the top of her head and tucked her head under his chin.

Another squeak came from the door as his friends, including Lily, joined them. Each was holding a missive from Tarleton, and that man slid in behind the others. He slowly allowed Margaret to break contact with him then searched his friends' faces and knew that it was time to leave.

"Let's go, shall we?" James asked before he took Margaret's hand and guided her out the door and down the dock to the ship that was awaiting them.

EDMUND SAT IN the carriage outside of Riverton House. The knocker was not visible at the door, meaning the viscount was not at home. Maybe Tarleton had indeed gotten Edmund's missive and not dismissed it. A rush of air came out of his mouth with a sigh.

"They don't seem to be at home," Edmund shouted out the door to the driver.

"Where would you like to go, sir?" the driver asked.

"We will need to go back to Saint George's."

For once in his life, Edmund didn't want to go back to the Priest's office. He knew what lay in store for him if the man found out that his mission had been thwarted. The Priest's right-hand man would be even more upset. Edmund shook his head.

"Change of plans, driver. Take me to the docks."

The carriage turned around and conveyed him to the docks. A man slightly shorter than he, and a good two stone heavier, strode toward the building that housed Riverton's shipping offices. His name was Matthew Lamont. Of Scottish descent, the man was big and had been a pugilist some years back.

Edmund knew him from those days. They had both been fighters and fought many times in underground bouts. They had been trained by the same man, who owned the establishment that Edmund now used to keep his skills up.

"Matt!" Edmund waved from the carriage.

The other man glanced up and smiled. "If my eyes don't

deceive me. Last I heard, you were missing somewhere on the Continent after Waterloo. What has brought you here?"

"I need to speak with Riverton. Is he here?" Edmund asked, hoping Matthew would give him a clue as to the viscount's whereabouts.

"I'm sorry to say that Riverton just left. He didn't say where he would be or when he would be back."

Edmund shook his head. The Priest was going to have him killed if he didn't bring Lily Thompson to him. *Goddamn it!* "You don't know where he went? Isn't that odd for him?"

Matthew glanced up. "All I know is that he and a group of others boarded one of the ships. I wouldn't know where they are going as a group. His lordship's sister lives on his Scottish estate. Maybe he would go there."

The only time Edmund had ever been to Scotland was to visit his aunt and uncle, who had a country house near Edinburgh. His mother's sister now resided in that house and would enjoy seeing him. Maybe, just maybe, he could find Lily before his life went to hell.

Since he was still in the Priest's carriage, a trip north was a possibility. "Driver, let's stop at my lodgings, and then we are bound for Scotland."

SEVERAL HOURS LATER, and with a missive to the Priest sent, Edmund was on his way to Scotland. He knew that the trip would take at least a week and a half. Depending on the weather, it could take two weeks or more. Thank the heavens that he had packed some books—and communications that he would post along his journey. A message to Tarleton was one of them.

He hoped that the driver didn't pay close enough attention when it came to his posting the letters. Yet something told him that the driver was not just a carriage driver but another agent, sent by the Priest to keep an eye on him.

The thought stopped Edmund in his tracks. Why had he not thought of this before? He could berate himself as much as he wanted, but nothing would change the fact that he was in a bad situation—worse than the one on the Continent.

It was just getting dark when they pulled into the first stop on Old North Road. The sound of drunken men singing crude tunes assaulted his ears. There was no way around it—he would need to procure a room for himself and make arrangements for the driver to bunk down somewhere in the mews, if the inn had them.

Edmund scurried out of the carriage and strode into the inn. The inside wasn't as worn down as the outside made it seem. There was a woman who sat on a chair at a counter, with numerous keys hanging on the wall behind her.

"Mistress, is there a room available for tonight?" he asked.

"Of course there is. I will have someone make sure the bed is turned down and made clean before you go up. You must be hungry. Our cook makes the best stew in town. Would you be wantin' a private room for your meal, or would you mind eating with the drunken louts?" the woman asked.

"I would much prefer the private room, please. I don't want my meal to be sacrificed to the gods of the bar brawl," he said with a smile.

"If you would wait here for a moment, I will make those arrangements. Did you bring a servant with you? If so, he can bed down with the other drivers in the mews behind the inn."

Edmund nodded in agreement as the woman left. He thought about going outside to have the driver move the carriage to the mews but thought better of it. He assumed that the man had already moved the carriage and was getting his meal and bunk.

A short time later, the woman walked back in and took her spot behind the counter. "Your room will be ready soon. If you would follow me to where you can grab a pint of our local ale and some stew…?" She smiled.

There was something about the woman that made him question this stop on the route to Scotland. They weren't three hours out of London and could've gone another hour or more before stopping. Sure, it would have been dark, but they would still have another hour's worth of travel under their belts.

The woman had something lurking in her midnight-blue eyes that caught him unaware—as if she knew exactly who he was and what he was doing. Her red hair and porcelain skin, with nary a freckle, reminded him of someone. He just couldn't place her. Was she a Shadow agent? An Order agent? Or was she one of Tarleton's?

As they made their way to one of the private dining rooms, the woman stopped and motioned him into the room then joined him. She closed the door and sat in the chair opposite him.

"Who are you?" Edmund demanded.

The woman stood and bent over the table. "I'm one of Tarleton's agents."

"Your name!"

"Abigail Cuthbert," she replied.

"How do I know you are who you say you are?"

"We worked together for a short time on the Continent. I kept you alive after your injury at Waterloo."

So, that was where he remembered her from. Edmund glanced at the woman again. It should have dawned on him that Tarleton would have someone at most of the stops along the Old North Road. The spymaster had enough agents, and with the war on the Continent over, he had even more spies in England happy for the work.

"Abigail, thank you for reminding me. Now, why does Tarleton have you posted here?" Edmund asked.

"My lord, there is a game afoot, a deadly one. Your driver is not who he seems. The spymaster told me to watch for you and to send word to Riverton's Scottish estate if you were to show up at this inn."

Again, it made sense, but this could be something altogether worse. Abigail could be a Shadow agent masquerading as one of Tarleton's. If Edmund was in London, he would have resources to guide him to a logical conclusion—but he wasn't in London. He was in some obscure town on the only major road from London up to the wilds of Scotland.

"I see you still don't believe me. I will leave you to your ale and stew. Find me when you are done eating, and I will show you to your room for the night," Miss Cuthbert said before she strode from the room, closing the door behind her.

The smell of stew wafted into the room as the door slid open and the meal was brought in on a tray. He thanked the young servant and ate the hearty stew in peace.

Chapter Sixteen

THE *ENDEAVOR* REACHED port several days after embarking on its journey to Edinburgh. James stood out on the deck watching the city come into view. The view never ceased to amaze him. Edinburgh Castle stood stoically on the top of a hill, overlooking everything in its domain.

He didn't have time to send a man ahead to procure carriages or coaches to transport everyone to his estate, Rosebriar House. Most of the men could ride horses that he kept in town for such an event, but he would need to ride in a carriage. He'd woken up with a stiff leg and found that a couple of the scars had reopened due to the shrapnel trying to escape their confines of the muscle in his leg.

Elijah and his twin brother, Silas, were also among the men that were asked to come along. Elijah held a marquisate somewhere in the Lake District but had left the estate in the capable hands of his land agent, and was also a doctor. Silas had been hired as a Shadow agent, but found the error of his ways and was now working for the Valor and Honor investigators. Their only sister, Amelia, was engaged to be married to Tarleton, of all people.

Thank goodness they had Elijah with them. James's family doctor was dangerous, as he believed in the old ways. The man had trained somewhere in England, not the famed school of medicine in Edinburgh. The man used bloodletting like a fiend. If you had a fever, bloodletting. If you had achy feet, bloodletting. If you cut your arm, the pixies did it. Each time he had called for the family doctor, he had to roll his eyes.

James had to laugh at the irony. If things had turned out differently... He shook his head. He didn't want to think about morose things.

"My lord, we are going to be docking soon. Would you like to take the helm, or would you like the captain to do it?" The bosun's mate clamored toward him.

It had been a long tradition for his captains and ships that if he was onboard, James would be at the helm when the ship docked.

"Not this time. Please tell the captain that he will be doing that today," James replied.

The bosun's mate bowed before pivoting toward the helm.

An hour later, the party was on their way to Rosebriar House. The house was just over a two-hour ride from Edinburgh. James knew that it was Margaret's first time to the house, and he hoped that the property pleased her. It was his favorite house in his vast holdings. Rosebriar was named after the climbing rose vines that wove their way up the house's façade. During the spring, the house was colorful. The extensive rose gardens were known throughout Scotland and parts of England. Lords and ladies were always wanting to visit the house or waiting for a house party to see the gardens.

Though that wasn't all they were doing in his gardens. Over the years, many couples were known to have gone into Gretna Green after having a tryst there. Luckily, he had never been caught in his pursuits of the fairer sex.

Next to him, Margaret was watching the scenery go by as the carriage lurched through the ruts in the road. One of these days, he would hire someone to fix the road. For now, the bumps drove him batty. Each bump had the pain in his leg nearly causing him to get sick. Damn and blast.

Just as he was about to suggest the carriage pull over, the beautiful red brick façade of Rosebriar House came into view.

The massive building stood at four stories high. There were four wings built around an interior court. It was home. It was where his parents had called home, where he got to know Ioan, and where his father and mother had died years ago from typhoid fever.

He leaned close to Margaret and whispered, "Welcome to Rosebriar House, my lady."

"It's beautiful," she replied breathlessly.

James smiled as he kissed her cheek. "This is home. My sister Grace lives here. There are a couple of things I need to tell you, based on the reception some of our traditions in these parts have had in the past. Have Matilda tell you about her experience.

"Back to the subject at hand, Rathdrum and I have protocol that if someone comes into the house without our knowledge, the bagpipes will be played as a security measure. They can be disturbing in a house this large because they echo. Do not be afraid. I promise that it isn't something bad."

"Bagpipes? Aren't they outlawed?" Margaret asked.

"They are, but that doesn't mean that the Scottish people don't play them where the English can't hear them." James waggled his eyebrows.

Margaret giggled. "You know I'm English, correct?"

"Of course I do, but you're married to a Scot." James winked.

The carriage lurched to a halt as it pulled up to the front stairs of the house. James got out of the carriage first and helped Margaret alight. He climbed a stair and instantly regretted doing so.

"It's your leg, isn't it?" Margaret asked.

James nodded. "Can you please go fetch Elijah? I'm going to need his help up the stairs and with my leg."

"I will be back with him in a moment," Margaret replied as she raced up the stairs.

Why hadn't he asked the doctors to amputate his leg? He knew why. He wanted to walk under his own power. He wanted to be able to ride again, play yard games with his sister, and play with his children—once he had them, of course. He felt weak, like an invalid, when he had these bouts of fever and the shrapnel protruding from his thigh.

Moments later, he heard the clacking of shoes rushing toward him. He looked up into the faces of Elijah and Margaret.

"Can one of you please help me inside? I need to sit down and rest before the good doctor extracts some of this shrapnel from my leg," James said.

MARGARET WATCHED AS Elijah helped James into the house and to a room near the front door. Obviously the room was used for invalids—a day bed had been placed near the windows, a small desk and chair were in the opposite corner, and no other furniture was in the room. Was this where James had convalesced while waiting for his leg to heal?

"My lady, would you please find a servant and have hot water and a bottle of scotch brought in here?" Elijah asked.

She didn't hesitate. As soon as she stepped out of the room, a large man dressed in livery stopped in front of her, holding a bucket of hot water.

"Cook figured the master would need this," the man said in a thick Scottish brogue.

"Thank you. I'm sorry, I don't know your name."

"My name is Hamish MacDonough," the man replied.

"Thank you, Hamish. Lord Riverton and I appreciate this. Please tell Cook thank you for me," she said with a smile.

It was obvious to her that the staff didn't know that she was the new Lady Riverton. That would be remedied soon, but she had more important problems to address—such as getting this water to the doctor.

"Would you like me to bring this in, my lady?" Hamish asked.

"Please. Doctor Elijah needs it."

Hamish nodded and strode into the room.

"Hamish, thank you!" came Elijah's voice from inside.

Margaret wished that she could be in the room with them, but being a female, she was not allowed to see what was going on. Instead, she figured she would stretch her legs a bit by touring the house. She stopped at an open door, about halfway down the hall, and stepped in. It was a parlor in pastels. A sewing basket sat next to one of the settees, and it occurred to her that this was Grace's domain.

"If you take another step, I will shoot you," came a female voice from behind her.

Margaret raised her hands in surrender and turned toward the voice. A short, delicate woman had both hands wrapped around a pistol, a finger on the trigger. She looked like a female version of James. Her blonde hair curled around her cherubic face, and her emerald-green eyes spat fire at Margaret.

"I would suggest putting the pistol down. I am here with your brother," Margaret said, hoping that her reassurance would calm the little termagant down.

"You're with James? He would've told me if he was coming with a female guest that I didn't know." The girl held the pistol tighter.

"James is down the hall with Elijah. You can ask him if you'd like."

"I will. Stay here or I will sound the alarm. Neither of us wants that," the girl said.

Margaret sighed as the younger woman lowered her weapon and stalked toward the room where Elijah and James were dealing with the shrapnel in James's leg.

"Grace, what in the…?" Elijah's voice echoed through the house.

"Who is the lady rummaging around my parlor? Is she one of the guests? And why isn't she with the others?"

Margaret had to hold back laughter when she heard the reply and the equally hilarious screech that came from her sister by marriage.

"Why didn't you tell me?" Grace asked as she raced back to where Margaret stood.

"I thought your brother may have written you about our marriage, but I figured that he didn't when you had the pistol aimed at me," Margaret replied.

Grace took a couple steps and embraced her. Margaret stood there in shock. How incredible that the younger woman's attitude should change so much with just one conversation.

"Matilda, Amelia, and I have a standing appointment in the long gallery upstairs, if you want to join us?"

An appointment for what? Did she really want to find out? Instead of asking the questions, she thought that maybe she should see what the other ladies were doing up in the "long gallery."

"I would like to see how you amuse yourselves in the long gallery," Margaret replied with a giggle.

"Follow me and find out." Grace skipped out of the room and ascended the stairs.

Whatever Margaret had thought the other ladies would do in a room called the long gallery, this wasn't it. In one corner, a table covered in blades of all kinds beckoned her. What was this? She touched a long blade, a dueling sword, and a claymore.

"Did I just walk into a dueling club for women?" Margaret asked.

"Something like that," Grace replied. "Each of us were trained to protect ourselves if something were to happen and the men couldn't be here. We also practice hand-to-hand combat. James taught me after our parents died and I was left in this rambling house with the staff." She picked up a small blade and ran her fingers over it in appreciation.

"Do the men know about this?" Margaret asked.

Margaret was already proficient in hand-to-hand combat and could probably teach these ladies a thing or two. She would take note of their abilities as they went through the drills.

"Of course they do. In fact, they prefer us to know how to protect ourselves if they are on missions. When they are away from us, they need to know that we will defend their homes and our lands."

"Shall we?" Margaret picked up some fencing gear and strode toward the middle of the room, taking the sword into her grasp and pulling on the face mask and vest. She swished the sword around and waited.

Margaret was not the least bit surprised when Grace took up a foil and gracefully engaged in a duel.

TARLETON HEARD THE clanking of metal against metal as he made his way up to the long gallery, where he knew the women trained. What he was unprepared to see was Margaret teaching some of her training to the other women. He smiled. He had spent a lot of time teaching her what she needed to know. Of course, her late fiancé had begun the training for him.

Margaret was his best assassin and agent. If he were to be honest with himself, he didn't want her teaching Amelia how to be an assassin. Not because she would excel at it but because he didn't want the love of his life to be part of that world. He should put an end to it, but he couldn't.

He smiled when Margaret and Matilda noticed he was there. They dropped their weapons and raced over to him. His niece and the woman that he had claimed as his niece launched themselves into his arms. He nearly toppled over when they reached him. Then Amelia followed, pushing the other women away. She lowered his head and kissed him.

"I missed you," she whispered.

"I was just downstairs, love. I needed to make sure that James wouldn't have an episode like he did a couple of weeks ago. He is recovering nicely downstairs in the hospital room." He glanced at

Margaret and shrugged nonchalantly. "It's what we've called it since James came back from Waterloo."

"If you don't mind, I want to go see for myself that he is healing." Margaret was clearly trying to not show her worry, but Tarleton put his arms around her, and she couldn't hold back the tears.

"You know that being strong doesn't mean you can't cry. Letting your feelings fester isn't the answer. Tears make humans out of all of us," Tarleton said loud enough for only her to hear. "Now, go to your husband. He needs you."

Chapter Seventeen

A WEEK LATER, Edmund finally made it to Edinburgh. The city was beautiful. The spring colors filtered out the gray and browns of the buildings. Edinburgh Castle highlighted the city, an imposing gem in the distance. From afar, his aunt's house had a view of the castle. He smiled as the carriage pulled into the house's circular drive.

His aunt was out on the steps waiting for him as he alighted from the carriage. It had been an age since he had seen her. She was still a beautiful woman. Her chestnut hair was streaked with gray, there were small lines etched next to her eyes when she smiled, and the cheerful laugh that he remembered raced toward him as he climbed the stairs.

"Edmund! My darling nephew, we were so worried for you. Why didn't you tell anyone where you were? After Waterloo, we thought you were..." She sniffled.

If there was one thing he was not comfortable with, it was a woman's tears. He held his aunt for a moment as tears dripped from her face to his shirt. He didn't mind—the shirt needed a good washing, since he barely had time to pack anything and had been wearing it for days.

"Auntie, I'm here and will be here for a while. My work is important, and I need to get up to Rosebriar House without my driver. Remember what my father used to do?" Edmund didn't want to say anything and have the household staff gossiping about him.

"Oh. Would you like me to distract your driver?"

He loved his aunt. Though he wished she didn't have to be privy to what he was going to do, he needed her help.

"Yes, please. Any distraction while I go to the stables to get a horse saddled and ready to ride would be helpful." He kissed his aunt's cheek. "I know I just got here, but I need to warn Tarleton."

"Lord Tarleton is in Edinburgh?" she asked in a whisper.

"He is with the Duke of Rathdrum and the Viscount Riverton. We need to keep that a secret, because there are innocents that need to be protected."

His aunt gazed into his face and nodded. "My darling nephew, I will distract the driver, but please, be careful."

"I will, Auntie."

What seemed like hours later, Edmund was able to escape from the driver's sight and ride northwest, away from Edinburgh. He needed to relay messages to Tarleton and to the Valor and Honor men, and he guessed the women too. He would have to send his thanks to his aunt for keeping the driver occupied. Some fancy baubles from Edinburgh or London.

His mind reverted to focusing on where he was. He had been to Rosebriar once before. He knew the landmarks, but he didn't consider that the trees may have fallen during a storm or had grown. The one thing he wouldn't miss was the Roman ruin where the road deviated from the drive.

The Roman ruin was said to have been where Saint Patrick was born. Though, to him, the name Maewyn Succat seemed more Welsh than Scottish. He shrugged to himself. He shouldn't argue with those who knew more British history than he did. Well, he could, and every chance he got, he did argue. He supposed that was why he got along with the neighbor girl where his parents lived.

Before long the ruin came into view, and behind it the red-brown façade of Rosebriar House made its appearance known.

He pushed his horse to a gallop and rode like the wind to get to the house. As he rode up, a large man waited for him.

"I need to see Lord Tarleton!" Edmund demanded as he jumped off the horse, handing the reins to a footman dressed in the Riverton livery.

"How do you know he is here?" the man asked.

"Along the route, a woman at our first stop told me he may be here at Riverton's estate. I need to speak with him before I am missed."

The large man nodded and motioned for Edmund to follow him. "They are in the library, sir. I will announce you."

They didn't get far before a shriek rent the air. "Oh my!"

The woman looked familiar to him. Could it be? His neighbor? "Margaret?"

"Yes! What are you doing here?" she exclaimed.

"I need to warn Tarleton. The Shadows are on the move, heading here as we speak. My driver is an agent, and I'm certain that he has been able to send word to other agents. They want Lily, and plan to kill her. I am also certain that they plan to kill me too."

"Why do you think that?" Margaret asked.

"It's a feeling I have. I felt the same thing before I got injured at Waterloo. A sense of foreboding. I can't explain it," Edmund replied. It was true. He couldn't explain how he knew that his time was nearly upon him. He had spoken with many soldiers before Waterloo, some that made it, and others that foretold their last moments. He felt such a foretelling now.

Just as Edmund spoke, a gentleman strode up behind Margaret and folded her into his embrace. In an instant, he knew the man to be the Viscount Riverton. The man was handsome and tall, hair swept back in the current style. His eyes assessed everything around him. Edmund could understand why his childhood friend—or should it be acquaintance?—had fallen for the man.

"Who is this, my love?" the man asked.

"James, meet Edmund Alexander. He has some dire news for Tarleton. I think we should all meet in the large parlor. That's just my opinion. We need to plan," Margaret replied.

Edmund bowed. "I can't stay long, but Margaret knows the majority of what I do. You have a day or two to decide. Rosebriar House seems like a defensible home. I would suggest arming all able-bodied men and women."

"Sir, we are Scots. We know how to prepare for battle against a damnable foe. We will survive, and they will rue the day that they came north!" Riverton exclaimed.

Edmund held back a guffaw. The man's exuberance made him believable. Unfortunately, his bravado may be lacking. He knew Riverton's service to the Crown. The man was a statistician and knew how to train a regiment to move from columns of four into lines of battle as easily as the next man, but could he manage to train his men, here on his own turf, to conquer a foe that could kill them as easily as any well-trained army?

"I need to go, unfortunately. I will see myself out." Edmund bowed and strode off.

"If you need something to occupy your time after this is over, please find Rathdrum. We will hold a spot for you," Riverton said.

Edmund glanced up at the viscount. "I don't expect to live that long, my lord, but if I come out of this unscathed, I will call upon the Duke of Rathdrum. I promise."

He tipped his head and walked out the door.

TARLETON TOOK A seat near the fireplace in the parlor, listening to Margaret relay what Edmund had said. They would need to open the arsenal that he knew Riverton had at Rosebriar. He also knew that Riverton's army of servants were well trained in case of an attack. Unlike the early days of the clans, there were no longer massacres, but the Clearances had brought back the need to protect the lands from English invaders.

Tarleton almost laughed at his faux pas. Riverton was a dragoon. He'd served the Crown, with distinction. Riverton had an army at his command to protect all within his reach.

"I think it's time to secure Rosebriar." Tarleton swiped his fingers through his hair.

Riverton nodded. "I agree. Brentmoor, my butler, will relay the message to the rest of the staff. He has the keys to the armory. I also have weapons in my apartments upstairs for us. I will have my men bring them down."

Tarleton was uneasy. Something wasn't right. The household staff were stilted. Could they have a Shadow agent in the house? God, he hoped not—for James's sake. It had happened to Rathdrum; the man's butler ended up being a murderer. Little surprised Tarleton anymore, but he supposed that he *could* be surprised—just not by the Shadows.

Chapter Eighteen

BRYAN JEFFERS COULDN'T believe his luck. The idiots had congregated in Rosebriar. He rolled his eyes. His nephew and his friends were predictable. Though, as a logical choice, Rosebriar was more easily defensible than the Rathdrum estate—unless you knew the secret way in. As far as he knew, Riverton didn't know about the secret passages or the tunnels beneath the house. He could get some men in and turn them loose on the Valor and Honor boys.

They were boys playing at being men. Trying to keep their women safe. They had four in their numbers, presumably with no special training between them. Yet he couldn't know for sure. Maybe the women knew how to kill.

Then he remembered who was in the house—Margaret Stapleton. Or, now, Countess Riverton. She was known throughout the Shadows and other spy networks as a highly trained and successful assassin.

The woman had over forty kills, mostly high-ranking French officers, under her belt. Other victims were agents in other spy networks. He couldn't help but admire the woman. For the time being, at least. He would be the man to kill her, to bring back her corpse for the Priest to see, before setting it on fire—or maybe dumping it in the ocean for the fish to feed from. He wouldn't waste his breathing thinking of possibilities, because she was in a highly defensible house—on a bloody cliff overlooking miles of the best farmland outside of England to the east, and ocean to the west.

Jeffers stood outside the small cobbler shop in the underground of Edinburgh. No sane man would come down here, but he wasn't a sane man. He was bloodthirsty and needed his next kill. Lily Thompson knew too much and was a loose thread that needed to be cut. The Priest had ordered it, and he would relish watching the lifeblood drain from Lily's perfectly pale skin.

Then he remembered his promise to himself while he was on the *Fury*. He would kill Riverton. He knew what was at stake—killing a member of the peerage. He couldn't get away with killing a duke, but he had no qualms about killing a viscount. He chuckled—well, more of an evil cackle.

"Sir, can I help you?" a gruff voice said, taking him away from his thoughts.

"Yes, I need some of your best men, and on the double quick, if you know what I am asking. Hopefully, some men who aren't afraid of killing or maiming men and women."

The gruff-voiced man took a moment to think. "I know of no man who would kill a woman. I will not help you."

"How about abducting them? Kill the men, steal the women." The Priest had only sent Jeffers a couple of men, not enough to wage war against Rosebriar. He needed more, and this was the only place he could trust.

"I could help you with that. I hope you know what you are doing. The news around town is that the Viscount Riverton has recalled all his servants and men to Rosebriar. I would be careful if I were you." The man bent his head and walked away. "I will have your men to you in the morning. I would advise you to rent a room for the night before trying to break down the viscount."

Jeffers would indeed need to rest before riding toward Rosebriar House. He knew that he was going onto the viscount's land blind. He didn't know anything about the landscape or the layout of the house. He knew of the secret tunnels, since Ioan's house was connected to Rosebriar. It was the quickest way to go from one house to the other. How else had he escaped his nephew's clutches for so long?

He couldn't get near Rathdrum Hall without the alarms being raised. He would need to find another way into the house. Maybe he would take a wee bit more time and round the harbor on a boat, a small skiff, to see if there were any caves. That idea held some possibilities, quite a lot of them. He wondered if they were defensible or if Riverton knew about any smugglers' caves.

He would sleep on his choices. Maybe by the time he woke up, he would have a plan.

MARGARET HAD NEVER seen anything as beautiful as the men and women parading in front of them in perfect formation. She had to hand it to James—he had trained his staff with the most care. She had witnessed their drills, and each one shot what they aimed at. She had originally thought that she would need to train them on how to handle a weapon—but no. They were brilliant. To be honest, *she* probably wouldn't be able to hit a target in the center with the weapons they had.

Not that James's weapons were much better. The hunting guns were clumsy and not the least bit accurate. She loved hunting with them but couldn't stand using them in a firefight. She couldn't imagine using one in a battle. Yet she knew that the Americans used what they had to fight—and they won against England. An army of farmers against the best-trained fighting force in the world, and the colonists won.

This little army was up against some of the most ruthless men that she knew. The Priest wouldn't allow a loss. He would kill his men himself or order it to be done, or maybe have them fall on their own swords.

"What are you thinking about, my love?" James asked as he crossed the room to haul her into his arms.

"I was thinking that your staff are awe inspiring. I've never seen such a thing in my life."

"From what I understand, the staff of Rosebriar have always been trained to protect the Viscount Riverton. My grandfather trained his men during the time of Culloden. The clan had decided not to fight in the battle, effectively keeping our lands safe. Though the English nearly took our land, our men and women stood by us to take fealty to the English Crown."

"That must have been hard to do, being Scottish." Margaret peered up at him.

"It was, from the stories I heard as a child. Secretly, we kept the traditions as much as we could. We play the bagpipes as an alarm. Ioan and Matilda have stories about the bagpipes that were played at Rathdrum Hall." James chuckled.

Margaret had heard the tale from Matilda. Unlike Matilda, Margaret had a love of the instrument. It gave her goosebumps. She couldn't help the shiver that raced down her spine.

"I've heard Matilda's story. She fainted or some such thing. I love the bagpipes. The only time I heard them was…"

"You best not say anything, my dear. I don't want my bagpiper to be hanged by the neck until dead. That's the punishment for any Scotsmen if they play outlawed pipes or wear the outlawed tartans."

She nodded. She didn't want any of her newfound friends and people to be turned in for doing something that was outlawed. She just might ask the bagpiper to play her something. She smiled.

"I might have asked your piper to teach me to play them," Margaret said in a singsong voice. She couldn't say she was all that shocked when James's jaw dropped.

"Oh, my darling wife, you have to stop or I'm going to have a seizure."

"I doubt that would happen, my lord. I promise I know how to revive you." Margaret winked.

Margaret did, in fact, know how to revive him. Her kiss was

all he needed. She would need to seduce him tonight. She hoped that whomever they were planning against would wait until morning to attack.

TARLETON SAT UP with Amelia reading in the library under the light of a candle. Seeing her so calm was against everything he knew about her. However, the serene domestic picture that formed in his head resonated with him. He wanted what Rathdrum, and now Riverton, had. He wanted it with every breath he took.

Then a voice from the hallway reached his ears. The most beautiful voice singing Robbie Burns's "(Oh) My Love Is Like a Red, Red Rose." The voice belonged to Margaret; she had performed the song at her wedding. Being here in Scotland, she was probably performing it for the staff. The keening of a violin joined her, and then more voices. Riverton's staff had joined in complete harmony. He sat there enjoying the performance from the library.

He knew from experience this would be the last performance for many of them. After tonight, they were on alert. The Shadow agents could be here at any time, and the staff were as prepared as they could be. Then it occurred to him that since they were on the cliffs, could there be smugglers' caves that either got to the house or were close enough to the house? One could be the end of them.

The library door opened and Riverton strode in. Tarleton needed to bring up the possibility of smugglers' caves and hidden passageways.

"Just the man I wanted to see," he exclaimed.

Amelia glanced up from her book. "I assume that I am going to either go up to bed or find a reading nook somewhere else?"

"No, my love. James and I will go to the study to have our

discussion. Please stay here and enjoy your book."

Tarleton stood up and followed Riverton to his study. The room was beautiful, in the masculine way that most studies looked. Though there were several windows in the room. The light during the day would be enough to work by.

"What can I do for you, Tarleton?" James asked, one eyebrow cocked.

"A thought occurred to me that we may not be as secure as we thought. Since we are so close to the sea, have we thought about what to do about smugglers' caves? Tunnels? Secret passageways?"

James broke into a smile. "The smugglers' caves have been sealed off for years. My great-grandfather allowed smuggling before the battle of Culloden. Once the battle ended, the need for smuggled goods continued, but with his truce with the English, he just couldn't maintain it. He lit a few charges and destroyed the network of tunnels leading to Rosebriar."

Tarleton let out the breath that he hadn't realized he'd held. One less thing to worry about. "What about secret passages within the house?"

"There is no way into the house without going through one of the doors. Of that, I'm sure," James replied.

"Then how did Jeffers make it from Rathdrum Hall to Rosebriar House without anyone seeing him?" Tarleton asked.

James thought for a moment. Then an epiphany struck like lightning. *Damn and blast it all,* he cursed himself. There were several other ways into the house.

"I had not thought of that. I will have the staff meet us in the grand hall. We need to find that entrance and post men there. How could I have not thought about that?"

Tarleton wanted to reassure the man, but they didn't have the time. They had to meet with the staff and change their plans—slightly, but change them nonetheless. "How many bagpipers do you have?"

"Well, most of the men are proficient in playing the pipes. I have them practice in the wine cellar, so they aren't heard by neighbors or guests."

Tarleton knew that was a feat all on its own. The bagpipes were an instrument of war, meant to be heard for miles. He was impressed.

"We need to have them strategically placed throughout the house and the perimeter of your property. Each station has a different tune they play. Can your staff do that?"

James nodded. "I believe they can. Let's go rally the men and women. Most of them are in the hall listening to Margaret as she performs some Scottish songs that she has learned."

Tarleton glanced at the other man. This mission was putting a strain on all of them, but he knew that James was taking on more than he should. The man should be resting his leg. The limp that James walked with relayed to Tarleton that the pain was extreme. He worried about his friend, but there was no way that James would sit this mission out.

JAMES WAS SHOCKED that he hadn't thought of the tunnels under the house that lead to Rathdrum Hall. He had seen the renderings of the house. He had forgotten about those damn tunnels. He shook his head. Thankfully, Tarleton had thought about it, or their defensive positions would have crumbled into dust in front of their eyes.

He thought through the possibilities. He had some masons who could erect a wall in a short time. He could collapse the tunnels, but that would risk the house, since the tunnels were directly under it. He could leave it the way it was and have a company of men down in the cellars to keep anyone out. Though that wasn't much of a possibility, since the bigger of the men would have to be in the hall to ward hold a breach at the front door. The women would be up on the flat roof acting as sharpshooters.

Thanks to his father, the women had become proficient marksmen—or markswomen? They were better than any man, and just as ruthless when it came to defending their homes. He had seen this one other time, and that was at Rathdrum Hall. He hoped that his men and women would do the same for Rosebriar.

The music that his wife performed stopped. She had finished her recital for his staff. It was time. He nodded at Tarleton, telling the man silently that it was time for them to discuss the change of plans.

He noticed that more than a few of his staff were walking away. "Please don't leave. Lord Tarleton has some changes to the original plans. How many of you know where the secret tunnel is that leads over to Rathdrum Hall?"

Ioan glanced up at him in shock. He didn't know about the tunnel. Well, that was going to be an interesting conversation later. James did not break eye contact with Ioan as Tarleton droned on about the changes they had discussed in the study. Once finished he dismissed the staff, James turned to Ioan.

"What do you mean there's a tunnel between Rosebriar and the Hall?" Ioan demanded.

"Did you ever wonder how Jeffers made it from the Hall to Rosebriar without anyone seeing? He didn't come by horse, and he didn't walk. There is only one way, and I had completely forgotten about it until Tarleton asked about the possibilities of something like that existing," replied James. He hoped that his friend would believe him.

"If there was such a tunnel, Matilda would have found it by now. She sniffs out secret passageways and tunnels like a dog. My wife found her way from her townhouse to my study through a secret passageway. While she was on the search for the next one, allowing her father in and out of the house without anyone realizing it, I followed her. The rest, as they say, is history. But I do believe that Matilda would have found it by now."

"Matilda would if she *knew* that there were secret passageways and tunnels in your house," James replied. "And it wouldn't be much of a surprise to know that there were. A priest hole in a house would need a tunnel to get that priest to safety. Would it be safe to say that the Archbishop of Canterbury has renderings of our houses and the Priest has had access to them? Or maybe he has intimate knowledge of your house?"

James knew that he was just rattling off scenarios, but that last one made sense. The Priest wasn't his priority now—that was keeping Miss Lily Thompson alive and putting Jeffers in a lead coffin, where he belonged.

"Let's go up to visit with Matilda," Ioan said. "She wasn't feeling well earlier, but hopefully she is feeling better now." The worry on his face relayed how "feeling not well" was an understatement of how the duchess really felt.

"Has Elijah been up to see her?" James asked.

"I believe he has and said that it was nothing to worry about. I took his word about it, but I can't help but worry. He didn't say what was going on, but James, I'm scared."

James saw the worry dripping from his friend's gaze. "If Elijah says she has nothing to worry about, I would believe him. He has helped me through most of the issues with my leg."

"I know. I trust Elijah with my life. I just want to know what is wrong with my wife."

Patting the duke's shoulder, James pushed the man toward the stairs. "Let's go up and visit Her Grace."

Chapter Nineteen

MARGARET, AMELIA, AND Lily were lying on the bed in Matilda's room trying their best to make the duchess laugh. The woman hadn't been herself the last couple of days. She had been withdrawn and spent more time in bed than was normal. Matilda's face was normally an alabaster, with a bit of a blush on her pale cheeks. That blush was gone, and Margaret could see for the first time that there were freckles on the woman's face.

Each of the women had noted the duchess's wan appearance. Every couple of minutes, Matilda raced for the chamber pot and threw up whatever she had eaten or, in some cases, hadn't eaten. They were worried. Margaret remembered that her friend didn't handle being on the water very well, but that wasn't what was going on. They had been on land for some time now.

Margaret watched as Matilda subconsciously moved her hand over her belly. Was she telling her something? Matilda nodded her head just enough for Margaret to see. Oh my! Did Ioan know? By the expression on Matilda's face, he did not. She would keep her friend's secret for now.

A knock on the door broke the trance that the women had been under. Margaret pushed herself off the bed and tiptoed to the door. She opened it, slightly, and noticed both James and Ioan standing out in the hall. The two men were too handsome—and serious.

"Have I found myself in the wrong room?" Ioan asked. His stern gaze frightened her.

"No, I believe you have come to the correct room. Matilda, Lily, Amelia, and I were having a party. You may come in."

Margaret noted the stern gaze turn to one of mirth—on both men.

"Matilda is well enough for company?" Ioan asked before he entered the room.

From inside the room, Matilda replied, "Maybe you should come in and find out for yourself, Your Grace."

Margaret giggled. Even though Matilda was ill, it didn't hinder her fun-loving nature.

"Well then. I will come in." Ioan chuckled.

Margaret had tried to tell Ioan and James that they were having a party, but seeing three women lying on their stomachs, whispering of God knows what, had both men laughing.

"What kind of party are you encouraging, Lady Riverton?" Ioan asked.

"The fun kind, Your Grace. Matilda was just telling us about the secret passageways in your townhouse. Did you know—"

Ioan cut her off. "Matilda, my love, have you found any secret passageways or tunnels in Rathdrum Hall?" he asked.

Margaret glanced at her friend. A slight blush stole across her cheeks, enhancing the paleness of her skin.

"My darling, what have you been up to? I spoke with Elijah earlier, and he said that I shouldn't worry about you, but I think that may have been a bit premature."

"I wanted to speak with my friends, Ioan. They are aware that I am not feeling well, but I still wanted to see them. I don't like being hidden away in a room without being able to speak with or see people."

Margaret felt Matilda's words to her core. Would James do the same thing to her if, or when, she became with child? It wasn't like they were preventing it from happening.

She smiled to herself, then pivoted and found herself in

James's arms. A brief kiss on the top of her head made her feel like the most treasured woman in the world. Not that she didn't think that Matilda didn't feel the same.

"Can you help James's men find the Rosebriar entrance?" Ioan asked Matilda.

"Of course. It's in the wine cellar. There's an out-of-place nook in the cellar—the weighted door is located there. Also, there's a sconce with no candle in it in the same nook; press down on it and the door will open." Matilda smiled.

"Ladies, let's give Her Grace some time to rest. You can come back in the morning if she is feeling well enough." The duke gave no quarter to the women remaining in the room. "Do I need to repeat myself? Please go to your rooms, and you will be able to have your daily practice time in the long hall tomorrow."

It was comical how quickly Amelia and Lily jumped from the bed and raced out of the room. Neither wanted to be on the duke's bad side. Margaret should have left as well, but she felt that she couldn't let her friend down by leaving. It wasn't until James cupped her elbow and guided her toward the door that she knew Matilda would need privacy to tell her husband the glad tidings.

She nodded and proceeded with James to their rooms.

THE NEXT MORNING in Edinburgh, Bryan Jeffers met with his men for the first time. The cobbler had kept his word and had twenty-some men for him to use. None of which were afraid of Riverton's army. If he were a God-fearing man, he might have feared the viscount, but he knew that the man was going to be prepared for his coming. That was the downfall of any plan. He just didn't know how prepared the man was.

Jeffers thought back to his man in the viscount's household. He hadn't heard a word from him in ages. He could only hope that by later in the morning, he would get a missive. Yet, if he was the viscount, he would lock down Rosebriar and keep all outside communications from gaining entrance to the people at the house. Going by that, he would assume that his man wouldn't be able to get the word out to him.

He also needed to add to his plans the possibility that the viscount and the rest of the Valor and Honor men knew about the smugglers' caves and the tunnel between Rathdrum Hall and Rosebriar House. Fuck! He couldn't win this round. It was the Valor and Honor men or the Priest who would finally end his life. Though he couldn't imagine another way to go. He deserved it for all the killing he had done throughout his career as an assassin.

His whole life flashed through his mind. He had, of course, murdered his own brother and three of his sons with a poison made with the plants in their very own garden. At the time, he had laughed that he had killed a man so highly thought of and so highly guarded. He had been the butler at Rathdrum Hall since he was a young man. His father had the old butler teach him everything a butler would need to know, and, somehow, without the son—his brother—knowing that Jeffers was the product of his father's affair with an upstairs maid at the Hall.

It had seemed that his life would go on as it was. Then one night, a young man came to the house. Jeffers didn't know the man, but he was draped in the robes of the clergy. A man of the church. The man came up to him and offered him a position with the Shadows, an organization that worked for the best of the Crown. He was trained on his days off, and when the duke, his father, had gone to England during the London Season.

He learned how to wield a gun, how to throw knives with precision, and how to fight with his hands. He would occasionally fight in the underground bouts in Edinburgh to keep his training up. That was where he'd met the cobbler, who was always at the fights. He would throw a couple of pounds sterling into the hat for him. When Jeffers won the fight, the man would put additional funds in the hat for him.

Even now, he had great respect for the cobbler. He didn't know the man's name, but he knew that the cobbler was a man of his word.

"Sir, we need to get going," one of his men, Robert, reminded him.

"We are going to split into two," Jeffers said. "One group will go by sea to Rosebriar. The others will come with me via Rathdrum Hall. Do not engage until you are signaled. We have already discussed the signal. If an attack happens without the signal, our offensive becomes a defeat. If you come across any of the women, do not harm them, but bring them to the ship and sail back down to Edinburgh." With that, Jeffers chose his men and left the others to get to the ship that he had acquired for their use.

For once in his life, he was not optimistic about this mission. The viscount had sixty-some well-trained servants, and he had twenty-four men of varying ability. His mission was doomed.

IF THERE WAS one thing Edmund remembered about his time at war, it was the sense of desperation in the air. He had made it back to his aunt's house in Edinburgh just two hours after leaving Rosebriar. He had made record time, and his poor horse had nearly collapsed at the stables. His aunt didn't question him, nor had she told him about the driver. He should have expected that the driver would be in his room waiting for him to return.

"My lord, you were gone for quite some time. Where were you?" The man's question seemed more like a demand. A servant wouldn't question his master. But Edmund was not the driver's master.

"I was up at the edge of the Rosebriar estate doing some reconnaissance. You don't think I want to go into this without knowing what I'm going into? If so, you are sadly mistaken. Now,

I need some rest, if you don't mind." He rushed the man out the door.

Edmund knew what his personal mission was, and that was to keep the Valor and Honor men alive to investigate the next mystery, and the one after that. His mission was to see that the women were safe as well. Knowing Margaret, she had already taught the women more in the days they had been at Rosebriar than they had collectively learned through their lives.

He disrobed and climbed into bed, knowing that the next time he went to sleep, it would be his last.

AT ROSEBRIAR, LILY couldn't sleep because the sun had already risen. No matter how hard she tried, she couldn't settle down. She forced herself from the bed, grabbed one of the candleholders from the small stand next to it, and went in search of the kitchens. What she really needed was a cup of warm milk—maybe that would help. Her nervous energy had been keeping her awake for days. She couldn't sleep, she couldn't read, and she barely wanted to practice her shooting, throwing, and pugilism.

She couldn't make herself do anything. As she meandered her way into the kitchens, she realized she wasn't the only one up and about early in the morning. She noticed the outline of the person. Doctor Elijah. She knew that without a doubt.

"Aw, my dear Lily. I wasn't expecting you awake this early in the morning. What brings you here?" the doctor asked as he continued doing what he was doing.

"I couldn't sleep and hoped to make some warm milk," she replied as she watched him ground some herbs in a small bowl.

"I see. I'm grinding some valerian root. It has some medicinal properties, including being a sleep aid. Would you like to try some?"

Lily didn't like taking some kind of root to help her sleep. She shook her head.

"If you don't mind, please use your words, darling. I can't see when you shake or nod your head," he told her. She didn't want to verbalize her response nor explain why she didn't want to use the valerian root.

"I don't want to use it, sir," she responded.

"That wasn't all that hard, now, was it? Lily, I would never force you to take any mixture that I may make in the future, but I would like you to tell me if or when you would like to. I have noticed since arriving here that you have been most anxious about what will happen next. I don't want you to worry about this. I promise Tarleton and the rest of them know what they are doing."

Lily nodded. "I will try, sir. Would you help me with the warm milk? I, personally, have no clue about how to make it. Mama was the one who always made it for me."

"Thank you for trusting me, darling. Now, watch me make it, so next time you can make it yourself."

Inside, she wanted Elijah to be in her life to make it for her. Why was he doing this? He had kissed her.

"Why are you treating me like a stranger?" she asked.

Elijah, finally, glanced up at her. "It's not that I think you are a stranger. I promise you that isn't the case. Until this mission is over, I can't think about what might happen to you in the next few days. If you are taken away, what would that do to me? It would hurt me to the core. I don't want you to think that I pursued you just because one of us might die in a firefight. No, darling, I wouldn't do that to you.

"Make no mistake, I want you, darling. Above all, I want you safe. Neither of us will be safe if we are distracted. That's why I am treating you as I am. We need to focus on what we are doing tomorrow and the days after."

Everything Elijah said made sense to her. She couldn't focus if she knew that Elijah was in a different part of the house than she was. She watched as he started making her the warmed milk.

Chapter Twenty

TODAY WAS THE day, Jeffers told himself as his men rode onto the grounds of Rathdrum Hall. It had been months since he had been here last. He sneered. His nephew had put him on a goddamned ship for a one-way trip to Australia, but he'd shown the almighty duke! The duke would never forget that Bryan Jeffers had escaped his punishment and returned to Scotland. The thought made him laugh. He would dearly love to see the duke look on in terror as Jeffers murdered every one of his friends and their women.

He and his men jumped from their horses and entered the house, kicking in the door. They made their way down to the duke's cellar and opened the secret door to the tunnel between the Hall and Rosebriar House. They hadn't sealed the door—that would make things better for him. He turned toward his men.

"You three." He pointed at the three men who looked like they could run the fastest. "I want you to go to Rosebriar House. Wait ten minutes and then race to the front door. There will be gunfire aimed at you. Once the shooting starts, the men from the cliffs will make their way toward the house, and the rest of us will be gaining entry to the cellars." He caught the worried look of the three men. "Once inside the house, dispose of anything that moves."

One of the three men spoke up. "I thought we weren't to kill the women?"

"I did say that, didn't I? Don't kill the women. The chances are they will be somewhere safe until after our firefight. The goal, gentlemen, is to capture the women and bring them to the Priest's country retreat near London. The men, you can kill at your convenience."

Jeffers couldn't help but laugh. The men were squeamish about killing women, but killing men was perfectly acceptable. He rolled his eyes and went about his part of the plan. He watched as the three men, whom he fully believed would not make it through the battle, raced off toward Rosebriar, and he led the other men down into the bowels of Rathdrum Hall. He found the head of the tunnel and strode with purpose down the long passageway.

JAMES WOKE UP early by his standards and gently nudged Margaret to wake up. "It's time. Get dressed and meet the rest of the women on the roof. For no reason should you come downstairs until one of us comes to get you."

Margaret nodded and stretched. Too bad he hadn't woken up early—he would have loved to have a taste of her before things started happening. Unfortunately, he didn't have that option this morning. He leaned over, kissed her passionately on the lips, and broke the kiss just as quickly as he had started it.

Then the sound of bagpipes wafted through the air. The tune told him that there was movement at the gate. Damn it!

"My love, you need to get upstairs soon!" he exclaimed as he raced to put on his clothes and run down the stairs.

James had a hunting rifle, several knives, his rapier, and his bayonet from his days as a dragoon. He knew how to use each of them in a lethal way. Anyone who wasn't one of his people would die a most agonizing death. He would make sure of that.

He had worried about Margaret but knew that she was nearly

as well trained as he was. James brought his mind back to what he needed to do. As he rushed down the stairs, he noticed his men scrambling to get to their positions. He had made sure that there were men at the entrance to the tunnel—ten, to be precise. He hoped they were ready for the onslaught they would be facing in a moment. He was worried that the masons hadn't erected the wall correctly and that Jeffers would bring explosives with him. The thought curdled his stomach. He hadn't thought of that the day before, and it hurt him to think that his men would be harmed.

It was too late to change course now. He raced for his position at the top of the stairs behind one of the big columns stretching from the hallway floor to the ceiling. He had a sharpshooter's position within the house, just like Margaret would have one in the front of the house, ready to shoot anyone coming in the door.

He had to hand it to Phineas. James had forgotten to have someone at the back door. Phineas had found a way to guard the door himself and still guard some of the other entrances into the house. Unfortunately, he was only one man.

James had been friends with Phineas since they were young boys at school, but he didn't know what the man did. There was speculation about what he was or what he did. Soon they would all find out how Phineas would handle the pressure and the fight ahead of them. James shook his head and brought his thoughts back to the present.

"My lord, they are about to breach in the back!" one of his men shouted down the hall.

Just as the man shouted, another bagpiper sounded the alarm. The tune told James that it was the back door, where Phineas was, that was about to be breached.

"Send some men there, quickly!" he commanded as he took up his rifle and watched the front door. Yet nothing came. Then the roar of a gun being fired rumbled through the hall. It was the women. Simultaneously, ten guns went off on the roof. *God bless the women,* James told himself, and he smiled, knowing that Margaret was on their side.

"My lord, it was the oddest thing! We were being overrun, and then guns were fired from above and they dropped like flies!" one of his men reported to him.

Communication was key on any battlefield, whether at home or abroad. "Thank you. Now go to the back door and defend it."

The man nodded and raced back to his position. Sometimes James wished that the men in his regiment had been as disciplined as the ones here and now.

He felt a rattling from below him. Then the unmistakable sound of gunfire. He needed more men in the cellar. His position wasn't needed any longer.

As he was racing down the stairs, he saw Phineas and Ioan rushing toward the stairs to the cellar. Tarleton followed on their heels. Why weren't they defending their positions? He got to the back door, and his jaw dropped in surprise. There was no one left to defend against. At the front door, Margaret had laid waste to the men who tried to break through their front. Jeffers had sent just three men to the front and at least ten or fifteen men in a flanking movement. Yet Jeffers was nowhere to be seen.

He was coming in through the tunnel—meaning that the mason's wall had succumbed to the man. Well, the battle for Rosebriar would happen in the darkness of the cellar. If that was the way the winds had changed, so be it.

TARLETON KNEW WHAT was coming before he saw it. When he saw Ioan and Phineas race toward the stairs down to the cellar, with every bone in his body, every breath in his lungs, he knew that Jeffers, the right-hand man of the Priest, was waiting for them. From the sounds of the gunfire in the room that they were about to enter, Riverton's men were putting up a fight. Against a crazed man like Jeffers? The men had a slim chance of making it upstairs to their families. They would need to end this…and soon.

"What are you waiting for? Get down these stairs!" Tarleton commanded the men, but realized that several bodies were barricading the way in. "Go around them if you can, but we need to get into this fight."

He knew that Ioan had very little experience in warfare. Phineas, on the other hand, was one of his best intelligence officers. Handy with a gun and ruthless with a blade, the man was skilled in keeping himself and others alive. That was Tarleton's goal—utilizing his secret weapon.

"Where do you want me, sir?" Phineas asked as he pulled several throwing knives from his secret pockets.

Tarleton glanced into the room to see Jeffers standing over one of Riverton's men, knife in hand, ready to kill the man in front of their eyes. "We need to keep him alive, for now. Take care of the other men. Aim to maim, not to kill. I need to question them."

Phineas nodded and snuck into the cellar along the shadows. Tarleton kept his eyes on the man. He would need to give him some time once this mission was completed. His family's estate was in sad need of repair and needed the laird of the manor to be home. Of course, Tarleton knew his own house needed repairs and management by the master.

Within moments, the only men who were standing were his own men and Jeffers. Tarleton sighed in relief. He looked up at the ceiling of the cellar and prayed for the first time since his sister's death in childbirth. The sound of bagpipes rose again, but in the same tune, letting all within the house and grounds know that the battle was over.

They had lost five men in the cellar. Five men dead. Tarleton shook his head. It could have been worse. The men and women of Rosebriar might not have been as ready as they had been. In the end, they had Jeffers and the hired men that he had brought with him in custody.

Chapter Twenty-One

MARGARET HEARD THE change in the tune that the bagpipes played. All they needed to do was wait for one of the men to let them know that it was over. Just then, James's head peeked at her from a window in the attic. His handsome face was a reminder that they were alive. They had made it.

"All's well, ladies. Let's get you all inside. We are going to need help getting the ones we've lost to the local minister. We will also need you to help with nursing the wounded back to health. I know that Lily may want to be there." James reached toward her. "I need to feel you in my arms for a moment before we get back to doing what we need to do."

Margaret knew there was nowhere else she wanted to be at that moment but in the arms of the man she loved with all her heart. Then it occurred to her—had she never told him how she felt about him?

She stared at him in the eyes and said, "I love you."

The smile that lit his face nearly blinded her, in the best way. The man chuckled as he lifted her in the air and twirled her around. She loved this man with every ounce of her being. There was no adequate way of telling him what she felt, so she lowered her head and kissed him, lovingly, passionately, and thoroughly.

From outside, clapping and cheering stunned them from their excitement for each other. Margaret knew in that moment that it would always be James and her. There was no one else for her. It was always him. Even years ago, it had been him.

"I love you too, darling. We will continue this later, much later." He winked as he guided her down the stairs into the house.

EDMUND HAD MADE his way back to Rosebriar after the fight took place. They had already started digging graves for those who hadn't made it. He'd tried to get to the house before the fight, but the soldier inside him knew that he would be seen as an enemy, and he had no wish to be shot by one of Margaret's guns. Friendly fire was, of course, the biggest killer on the battlefield.

He was at Rosebriar to see that Jeffers would make it to the noose this time. He would make sure of it. Come hell or high water, that man would feel the bite of the rope around his neck, and Edmund would be there to see it or do it himself.

It had been, at least, a month since he had seen the deranged man. There was something inherently wrong with him. His need for blood—he was desperate for it. Edmund had never been around a man quite like Jeffers before. Though he had been around killers, he had never been around one that *needed* the kill more.

He wondered if it was bred into the man's family. Though what he knew wouldn't support that, since the current Duke of Rathdrum was Jeffers's nephew, and Ioan Rathdrum didn't seem deranged. If he was, Edmund would eat his own shoe.

He watched as Phineas and Ioan ushered Jeffers up the cellar stairs. The man had been gagged. In normal situations, the treatment of a prisoner was subject to negotiations in the army or the Royal Navy. In this case, the man was a risk to have alive. As deranged as he was, he could try to assassinate the king or the prince regent. Edmund saw the man drop, dead weight in the hands of the two men.

Within moments, Jeffers pulled a pistol from the inside pocket of his coat and pointed it at Ioan. Edmund ran toward the duke and tackled him to the ground. He heard the sound of the pistol firing and felt the burning pain of lead meeting his flesh. Darkness tried to pull him under when another report of a pistol joined the echo of the first. He watched in curiosity as Jeffers fell to the floor lifeless, a penny-sized hole in his forehead.

Edmund grabbed for his stomach, trying to staunch the bleeding, but it wasn't stopping. He had been shot before, but this was much more serious. He heard someone say, "Get the doctor!" and succumbed to the darkness.

ELIJAH, WITH LILY in tow, rushed to Edmund. The man was gut shot. There was nothing he could do. Even if he sewed the man up, the chances of making it through the night were not in his favor. Elijah hadn't known the man, but he had stopped the assassination of the Duke of Rathdrum, who had become a friend of his.

"Isn't there something you can do?" Lily asked, tears streaming down her face.

His sweet Lily had a large heart, and being a doctor's wife may be too much for it. Elijah still needed to romance her more before that happened.

"There's too much blood, my sweet. He may not wake up. It is better to say your goodbyes now. He should still be able to hear you." He knew that there wasn't much comfort to his words, but it was the truth. He watched as Margaret also heeded his words and dropped to her knees to say her goodbyes.

Elijah knew that the man was a good one, and that he would be missed. He wished that he could do more than just make the man comfortable and watch him die. Maybe someday, he would be able to repair damaged organs and flesh. Tears seeped from his eyes as he watched his friends and family crowd around the dying man.

It was moments later that the rattling breaths stopped and Edmund passed into the next life.

Epilogue

I T TOOK THREE long weeks for the Priest to learn of his brother's demise. He shouldn't be surprised at Bryan's death. The man had needed someone at Bedlam, but he got the job done, and that was all that the Priest needed him for. What else was an illegitimate brother good for? Ultimately, the man got what was coming to him.

The only problem he foresaw would be that his nephew was still alive. It made him furious that Bryan had killed Edmund and not the do-gooder duke. He rolled his eyes. Lily was still alive as well, and that had to change. The Valor and Honor Investigators would know that he knew where she was, at Rosebriar, and they would have to move her to another location before the Priest could get to her.

He stood up from his desk and strode toward the closet where Lily used to change into her boyish attire. He smiled sardonically. Oh, he would find her. It seemed like the men had a tell. The Baron of Strathmore Phineas Stanton's Scotland estate would be next—he would bet on it. Or maybe they would come back to London. He had a mission for his new protege.

He yanked on the bellpull thrice to signal his footman to come to him. Moments passed. Normally, the footmen were quicker than this. Finally, the door opened and a large man came into the room. His sun-darkened skin made him seem older than he was. Was this the privateer captain that had owed Jeffers a debt? If so, the Priest could use the man and his ship to do his bidding.

"Sir, I am Captain Mayhew of the *Fury*. I need to speak with Mr. Jeffers. Is he available?" the man asked politely.

He obviously had no clue who the Priest was and why he should be scared. If the man had made it through a cruise on a boat for months with Bryan without wanting to kill the man, the Priest couldn't help but respect the good captain.

"I'm afraid Mr. Jeffers has passed on. Is there something I can help you with?" He sat back down in his ornate chair behind his desk.

The captain swore softly under his breath. "I needed to borrow from him to make it back to Baltimore."

"I see. With my brother dead, unfortunately, he can't help you with that. But I, on the other hand—I can help you out for a price." The Priest cocked an eyebrow and stared at Captain Mayhew. There was nothing stopping him from letting the port master know that there was an illegal ship in his port.

"What is the price?" The man obviously didn't know what to call the Priest.

"I need some cargo moved from Scotland to the colonies—oh, I mean the Americas. Would your ship be able to do this?" the Priest asked, drumming his fingers on his desk.

"Depends on the cargo. I do not deal with human cargo."

"Ah, you are one of those people, are you? Wilberforce has too much influence on the younger men and women of this country." The Priest pounded his fist onto the oak desk in front of him.

"I've only heard of Wilberforce in the papers. I've never seen or heard one of his impassioned speeches. I would like to," Captain Mayhew replied.

"Back to our agreement—would you like the money or not? I will give you five minutes to think about it. Until then, I am going to have a finger or two of whiskey." The Priest pushed himself from the chair and crossed the room to the mantel, where the decanters were beckoning him to drink. He grabbed the decanter of whiskey and two glasses. He poured two fingers of the liquid into each of the glasses and handed one to the captain. "Have you made your choice?"

"I have. I will take your cargo to whichever port in the Americas that you want, but I want to be paid up front. Deal?" The captain offered his hand to the Priest.

In the palm of his hand, he held the list of "cargo" that the good captain would be ferrying to the colonies. "If you don't mind, here is the list and where I would like them to go, and here is a draft for the money you will need to get you back home. I need to get some work done. Please leave and close the door on your way out."

CAPTAIN PHILIP MAYHEW knew that he had been fooled. He opened the list of people he was to sail home with. He tilted his head back and shook his head. He was against slavery of any kind, and what he was taking these people into was slavery. He knew a couple of the names. Why the man wanted these people disposed of in this way was truly beyond his reckoning.

There was one person on the list that he had previous knowledge of. Lord Tarleton? The English spymaster and entrepreneur? If Philip remembered correctly, the man was up in Scotland. He could make it in a week or two, depending on the wind and weather. It was mid-spring, but Lady Luck was never in his favor this time of year. He would have to guess two weeks' travel time, and another two hours from Edinburgh to the estates of the Duke of Rathdrum and the Viscount Riverton.

He continued to think of how he was going to get up to Edinburgh when he spied the next name on the list—Phineas Stanton, the Baron of Strathmore, his English cousin.

If you want to find out what happens to our valiant heroes and heroines, stay tuned for the next book in the Of Valor and Honor Series, *It Happened One Knight*.

About the Author

I am a single mother from Minnesota to a little boy. When I'm not working or playing with the "Little Pirate Lord", I'm writing my next book. I have books in two different series, right now. Ironically, the characters in my Wellesley/O'Brien Saga are the descendants of the characters in my Rakes and the Crown Series. I am also playing with a mystery series that may be part of the same family.

Social media links:

Facebook Author Page: facebook.com/JessicaAClementsNavarro

Facebook Reader Group:
facebook.com/groups/2497384330578831

BookBub: bookbub.com/profile/jessica-a-clements

Goodreads:
goodreads.com/author/show/18576993.Jessica_A_Clements

Twitter: twitter.com/JClementsauthor

Instagram: instagram.com/jessicaanneclementsauthor

Website/newsletter: www.jessicaanneclements.com

Amazon: amazon.com/~/e/B01LZNFGST

www.ingramcontent.com/pod-product-compliance
Lightning Source LLC
Chambersburg PA
CBHW071428300726
48976CB00004B/1272